What People are Saying...

A great novel not only tells a good story; it leaves the reader with a better understanding of the story's topic. Karen Biery's extensive research into slavery and the Underground Railroad through primary resources is evident on every page of *Chattels* as she vividly recreates scenes, characters, and events from America's darkest time. Abolitionists faced the loss of property and life in their quest to help fleeing slaves forever escape bondage. Slave owners stopped at nothing to retain their human property and protect their way of life. The inhumanity of the brutality of punishments meted out to runaway slaves if captured was horrendous. The indomitable yearning to be free and the endurance necessary to achieve freedom was testament to the strength of the human spirit. Salem, Ohio was a major battleground on the road to the Civil War and Ms. Biery has given us a rich, authentic, and memorable history lesson of courage, determination, and love, and the triumph of good over evil.

~ George W. S. Hays, Retired Librarian

Chattels

Karen Biery

Library of Congress Control Number:

ISBN — HC — 978-1-937958-24-4
ISBN — SC — 978-1-937958-25-1
ISBN — EB — 978-1-937958-26-8

Published by River Road Press

To all who are poisoned
by the disease
of prejudice.

Other works by Karen Biery:

believe, River Road Press

pieces, River Road Press

Coming Spring 2013 – *speakeasy*

Foreword

The idea of this tale came to me after reading several letters by Gertrude (Trudy) Whinnery-Richards-Brown recalling her father, Dr. J.C. Whinnery, and his involvement in the Underground Railroad in Salem, Ohio. Although Trudy and I never met, we shared a love for the same historic home on Jennings Avenue. In her correspondence she relived Dr. Whinnery's stories of slave smuggling. She shared that her father's iron rod, used to free slaves from a railcar, was "secreted" on her property though she was never able to find it (nor was I), but her vivid recollection of his experiences spurred my imagination.

The novel's progression captured and became my encapsulated thoughts on so much more than the travesty of slavery – it has forced me to examine my inner feelings and prejudices. Even the very title, *Chattels*, sticks in one's throat when verbalized. The word, which by definition denotes property, was a reference to slaves in the mid-1800's and its vocalization resonates shackles, chains, and iron. It is reminiscent of all that should have not been.

This journey began as an innocent return for a prequel to my first novel, *believe*, sprinted over the finish line, and ended as a story to stand alone. Although a few of my readers' burning questions are answered within its pages, my hope is that all who read it will be left to wrestle their own private conflicts.

I must first start by explaining that this story is mainly fiction. Although many of its characters are representative in nature, some were true resemblances of the lives that they led the fight to abolish slavery. The main individual who should stand apart is Daniel Howell Hise.

Daniel was a fervent believer in many things. He was an active member of the Women's Suffrage Movement. He opened his home to many diverse people—Frederick Douglass and Sojourner Truth, just to name a couple—and valued long debates with his visitors. He enjoyed Halloween and was known to hold séances or "spirit rappings" in his sitting room though he stated that he didn't really believe in it. He was an accomplished businessman, blacksmith, contractor, and steamboat engineer. He owned and operated a sawmill and a mercantile geared toward agricultural products, as well as a brick manufacturing company. His masonry work is still visible today within the Trinity Block in Salem, Ohio. He was a political activist and took a fervent stand against voting until Abraham Lincoln signed the Emancipation Proclamation. He was a respected Quaker, loved his wife and daughters, adored his country, and hated slavery.

Daniel moved into his farmhouse surrounded by 189 acres on Franklin Road (now Franklin Avenue) in Salem, Ohio in 1857 and immediately began to add onto the home until its completion in 1861. In my opinion, the reconstruction of this home spoke silent volumes of his stance on slavery. The home was more than doubled in size and built with underground tunnels, rooms that remained hidden, and trap doors to walled-off rooms or to the rooftops for a quick hiding spot or getaway. It had recessed doors that were camouflaged by furniture, windows that led to hidden rooms, doors that led to nowhere, and connecting closets for easier undetected movement. It boasted of six staircases, seven outside doors, and over fifty windows. "Unserheim" was a labyrinth of genius architecture built for only one purpose — to aid in the movement of slaves toward freedom. When its construction was complete, Daniel was embarrassed at its grandeur. If he only knew how many lives he would save, how many people would taste freedom because of his passion, he may have looked upon his German-named "Our Home" as a blessing rather than a lavish structure.

Daniel's tragic death of a presumed heart attack on November 21, 1878, left a large hole in the hearts of the townsmen of Salem, but his diligence to record 31years, 10 months, and 21 days of his life will be treasured for generations to come. His six volumes, beginning on December 26, 1846, and ending in November of 1878, can be purchased through the Salem Historical Society and are well worth the time to read their messages.

This novel tells the tale of a slave named George and his perils of travel toward freedom. It is not only about his personal tragedies, but also about the lives of so many unnamed people who gave of themselves, their property, reputation, loyalty to country, and religion, to help those less fortunate. Many stories have been told of the atrocities that befell the people who were simply born with a different color of skin, but few have been shared of the people who stood between death and life to aid in their freedom. I am speaking of the men, women, and children who felt the calling to make their home a "safe house."

I was in the midst of chapter six of this story when I contacted David Shivers, president of the Salem Historical Society, to ask for help with the name of a "real" blacksmith that I could plug into my novel. (For those of you who do not know, I like to incorporate real places and real people into a fictional story to make history come alive.) David put me in contact with Judi Allio of Salem, and she sent Daniel Hise's diary to me. I became engrossed in his life and reworked a few of the details that I had written earlier. In the entries of Daniel's diary in July of 1849, a random name began to surface – George. The hair stood up on the back of my neck as Judi helped me to realize George was a slave that Daniel had helped smuggle and who decided to stay in the area. In Daniel's diary, George assisted around "Unserheim". He hauled chips with his blind mare, painted the shop as well as buggies, and ran errands for Daniel. On February 5th of 1850, Slave Holders came to Salem, Ohio to hunt for George. Daniel wrote that he secreted George in the "country" until the excitement was over. (Many feel the "country" was the Jonas Cattell home on Jennings Avenue in Salem.) For those of you that have read *believe*, that was the home with the hidden room behind the fireplace — a *real* place of history in Salem.

Why did I interject this story here? To let you, my readers, understand how encoded this novel's foundation was. Think about it — I had already written about a slave named George knowing he was going to end up in Salem to tie this prequel to *believe,* while never realizing George was a real slave that had traveled in those very footsteps a century earlier than my fictional tale. I was unknowingly writing about a man and his story that had already happened. When Judi and I realized this coincidence, we were awestruck. I took that as another "God Wink" (thanks again, SQuire Rushnell) that I was on the right path and this novel had to be finished and shared.

My hope is that after reading this work of "fiction" you will look at those of a different race or religion as equal, worthy, and treasured for their ancestors who either were hidden to acquire freedom or were the ones who did the hiding. May these words ease thoughts of prejudice and judgment. After all, it is not our decision which color of skin we are born with, is it?

Acknowledgements

I must first thank Judi Allio and George Hays of the Salem Public Library who found the strength to decipher Daniel Howell Hise's diary. It was no ordinary task, but without their tenacity this tale would undoubtedly be much different. Following that historic vein, I am very grateful for the friendship and resources available through the Salem Historical Society. Their commitment to share history with the public is a treasure and an inspiration. Bonnie Rickman deserves to be named as the one who shared Trudy's letters with me long ago. Who would imagine that in sharing her love for the same historic home these thoughts spurred the story to follow?

I want to acknowledge how grateful I am to Barb Karlen for sharing Adah's Bill of Sale and daguerreotype with me and granting the privilege to copy them to share with my readers. Her true story was so relevant to this tale. Also, I am obliged to John Zamora and Kevin Schafer, the current owners of Unserheim, for my private tour. The information they shared was invaluable to this story. To be able to walk, crawl, and experience the slave's hiding places is something I will always cherish. Thank you both for being such willing and gracious hosts. Your love for history is evident within your home.

As always, I thank my husband Jeff for his untiring love and belief in me, and to my parents, Max and Evelyn Newton and Bob and Laura Biery, for their enthusiastic love and support. To my family — Annie, Adam, Ashley, Brian, Tracy, Kellie, Vicki, Jill, Aunt Carol, Aunt Barbara,

Tyler (for his beautiful foot), John and Barb — and friends — Sandy, Pat, Sue, Gwen, Tina, Patty, Elaine, and Shivers — who have eagerly cheered me on to the finish line. Thank you. I love you all.

I am so thankful to those that have helped with the editing and reading process — the always dynamic duo, Bill and Jean Esposito; the untiring Sue Stitle; my honest and talented buddy, Gwen DeCrow; Daniel's experts Judi and George; my long-time honest ally, Sue Forkel; and my treasured 'I must have a happy ending' friend, Pat Riley. Without all of your time, effort, and enthusiasm I may have lost faith.

My newly found life's work has given me great pleasure to blend my watercolors, photography, and the interior drawings with my love of words, and I am eternally grateful to all of you, my readers, for sharing this experience with me. Your support from our local area to national and now multiple countries is echoed through the Karen Biery Fan Club on Facebook. Your kind encouragement is humbling and makes me smile on a daily basis. Thank you from the bottom of my heart.

Prelude

On the following pages you will find a copy of an actual Bill of Sale for a slave named Adah Carter. On June 15, 1827, Adah and her two sons, Nelson and Americus, were sold to Samuel Palmer. Samuel paid four hundred dollars to slave master Joshua Potts of Loudoun County, Virginia for the rights and heirs of Adah. Samuel then set Adah and her sons free.

I smile when I read between the lines of the overzealous words relinquishing the claim of present and future rights to any heir of Adah's to be returned to slavery. The repetitive '…and all and every other person and persons whatsoever…' makes my heart leap for Adah and her children. The notion that a man would spend four hundred dollars for a slave family and then set them free is a triumph for the human spirit…

Adah Carter.

…and joy covers her face.

It is rare that a slave would be photographed. It is difficult to know when this image was taken — perhaps it occurred sometime after the date of 1827. In the margin of the document it is written that Adah lived in Belmont, Ohio after being freed. To me, Adah looks a bit older than 26 years old, though with the portrait's quality it is uncertain. But what is clear is her smile. Look at it. She is **proud**. She is **relieved**. She is **happy**.

And she is *free*.

1

I t was a cold Thursday morning. Abigail held her growing sides as the baby kicked within her. She fingered the edges of the note from her husband:

Will return as soon as able. Stay warm and well.
                    As always,
                    Nathaniel

She had read his penned words for the ninth time that morning. The warmth of his love enveloped her thoughts and shoulders. A thin smile crossed her face.

Immediately she doubled over in pain. She drew in her breath with short, strong gasps through her teeth. She exhaled slowly and repeated the process as her labor pains continued. She paced across the bare kitchen floor. The sound of her house shoes echoed throughout the empty house. Her pain lasted nearly ten minutes. Slowly she removed her hand from the edge of the gathering table. She waited nearly a minute before attempting to move her feet.

With her body relaxed she walked to the hearth and tossed the last two split logs on the fire. Her eyes traced the snow as it began to show its visible layers on the front porch. She knew it would not be long before she would be unable to access the outside world.

She struggled to move her swollen legs into her husband's spare set of wool underclothes and nearly lost her balance twice. Sharp needles traveled though her body. The baby kicked her ribs in revolt. She released the pain through a long, loud scream. Her child relaxed in submission.

Finally dressed in her husband's layers, she walked out the front door. The drop in temperature from the day before stole her breath. Four inches of fresh snow had gathered onto the edge of the porch floor. Careful not to overstep, she moved her feet wisely. One narrow stride at a time, she made her way down the set of four stairs to the frozen earth.

The snow skirted her knees as she pushed her way through. Each move was more difficult than the last. By the time her fingers touched the woodpile, she could barely catch her breath. The baby lay eerily still.

If she hadn't been nearly paralyzed by nerves, the blizzard of 1845 would have appeared breathtaking. The wet snow gathered thick on each tree limb. The long boughs of the pines caressed the ground from the extra weight. Each cloud layer built upon the last until the bottom stratum seemed to touch the mounding snow. Her world was still, oppressive, and lonely. Time seemed limitless.

Abigail struggled to crunch through the thick layer of ice that lay hidden a foot below the evening's storm. With each step she grew weaker. She managed to carry three loads of wood to the front porch.

In the frigid temperature she peeled off the extra layers of her husband's clothes. Snow clung to the fabric in heavy lumps. The garments fell to the porch floor with a thud.

She walked in her wet stocking feet to the hearth and tossed another log on the blaze. It fizzed and popped. The melting snow slowed the fire to a soft burn. With her drenched clothes splayed on the hearth, she collapsed in the fireside chair.

Sharp pain twisted her face. Instinctively, she grabbed her sides. She rocked slowly and tried to hum but found it too difficult. She placed her head back on the chair and tried to relax. Her hands massaged her protruding belly.

"It's too soon, my child...too soon," she whispered.

The baby was not due for another month. She silently prayed for her husband's safe and rapid return. She bent her thoughts towards Nathaniel to bid his homecoming.

Nathaniel rode hard through the night. He carried a hand-wrought iron rod in his left hand and the horse's reins in his right. He struggled to hold the bar steady. Occasionally it slapped the side of his steed and caused Kit to run with renewed fervor. He did not bother to slow him.

He arrived at Daniel Hise's blacksmith shop at nearly eight o'clock. The sound of clanking metal surrounded the structure. When Nathaniel rounded the corner, he found Daniel hard at work.

Smoke encircled the barn's hand-hewn beams as the fire smoldered. A faint shade of red glowed from Daniel's rod. He placed the flattened edge on his anvil for the last time and hammered each side with three blows. He blew the darkened pieces to the floor and thrust the rod's hot tip into a bucket of water. The water sizzled from the heat. The steam seemed eager to mix with the building layer of wood smoke. Daniel glanced at Nathaniel and quickly pulled it from the water.

Without a word, Daniel jumped on the back of his black mare and joined Nathaniel. They traveled across Daniel's open field and jumped over the hedgerow. The horses stopped on the opposite side without command. They walked in single file among the Osage orange trees to camouflage their tracks. Their movement was slow, yet deliberate. They exchanged no words.

After nearly a mile they changed their direction and headed northwest. Daniel whistled a low signal. The men looked to the edge of the field. Two others joined them. Their horses snorted in recognition.

Their path continued for nearly an hour. The horses obeyed their riders' silent orders. The men gathered their black cloaks around their bodies to shield them from the driving snow. Soon their tracks would be completely concealed.

Hanna drummed her hardened nails on the wagon's seat. Her hatred for the freedom fighters kept her uncovered hands warm. She glared at her driver. Her lips curled in a heavy sneer.

"They will be here, my lady. They will come."

"For your sake and the souls of your babies you *better* be right!" Her mouth snapped closed.

Joseph tried to explain, "I told them the train arrives at half-past nine. We've tracked them three times. They will travel this way."

Hanna Prenstrum scoffed at his words. She had little tolerance for tardiness, especially when so much was at stake.

She spit at him. "On your life," her eyes narrowed to signify business. "Your word."

"My word, Ma'am, my word. They will come."

They sat still in the snowstorm. The layers of white blanketed them covering their intentions. They bent their ears for any approaching sound.

Slowly two men rode along the edge of the field. Their cloaks were white. One man slid from his horse and approached Hanna's wagon.

"We are ready." He swung his wrap open to reveal his metal rod; its tip was broken. He pointed to the south. "Four men are in position there." He moved his pointed finger in the opposite direction. "And two are gathered in the thicket."

Hanna's eyes followed his directions, yet she made no sound. She followed his placements once again and nodded in agreement. She drew her timepiece from her pocket and scoffed at their lack of punctuality.

"The storm…," he began.

Hanna held her hand in the air to silence him. Her trembling hand pointed toward his horse. Without words, her order was clear.

He obeyed her command and returned to his horse, brushed the gathering snow from his saddle, and jumped on its back. The horse snorted and pawed at the ground. The rider squeezed his knees to silence him. All eyes settled to the far edge of the field.

Three others joined Nathaniel's group. The band of seven moved through a small patch of woods, crossed a frozen stream, climbed up a steep embankment, and stopped at the edge of a large open field.

One of the new riders rode to the leader. His whispers were barely heard over the wind.

"I think we need to double back."

"But the train arrives in less than an hour."

"I have a growing feeling of dread, Nathaniel. The field moves in clusters that should not be there." He pointed to the far edge of the field.

Nathaniel tried to shield his eyes from the blinding snow. His nervousness mounted while his vision and senses lacked. He struggled to focus on the faint movement of unknown objects.

"Please, Nathaniel, I know this field." With a tone of insistence he added, "We *must* double back."

Nathaniel's hesitation was brief. Convinced the clusters of movement were not spent chaff, he turned to follow the rider's advice. With his last backwards glance, he saw a single rider in the distance move to a settled position. His heart raced at the near disaster.

They moved back down the bank and followed the stream as it wound through the woods. The terrain was rough and movement was grueling. This path was not the chosen one, yet it was necessary to avoid the ambush that awaited them on the other side of the expanse.

With the final push, the men arrived at the railroad tracks nearly a mile from the station. They separated into their respective positions without direction. ``Only ten minutes had passed when the train's announcement was sounded.

Nathaniel watched the train slow as it closed in on the stocking station. With the final thrust of steam, the metal cars settled to a stop.

Nathaniel slid from his horse and ran along the rail cars. He moved his well-fashioned rod into the slat between the double doors of the nineteenth railcar and waited.

The dockhands worked by the light of a lone lantern. The watchman held the only other light on the opposite side of the train. His eyes peered into the darkness searching for any unwanted movement. From the front of the train only the first ten cars were visible, but the mounting snow prevented his advancement for a better view. He held his breath as he listened for any unusual sound.

Nathaniel held his arms steady waiting for the right moment. He heard the shuffling of feet from inside the car. He dared not speak.

As the first load of replenished coal was dumped, he forced the rod against the door. With a loud crack it flew open. The wide eyes of a black face stared at him in disbelief. Nathaniel held his finger over his mouth as an order of silence. The slave obeyed.

He jumped out of the car to the ground and settled into a foot of snow. He had no shoes and wore only a thin tattered shirt. Nathaniel helped the man onto his horse and covered him with a thick black cape while another rider held the door. Within a matter of minutes the cars rattled from the release of the second load of coal. The door was closed under the blanket of sound. The timing was perfect. The men saddled their horses and returned the way they came.

Nathaniel rode with Daniel. He shielded himself from the driving snow as they rode hard over the path they had made barely an hour before. Relieved that all had gone as planned, his thoughts moved to Abigail. A hot jolt shot through his body. He lifted his eyes and whispered a quick prayer.

After they crossed the stream, the group stopped. A thick blanket of steam covered the horses. Daniel pulled an extra pair of boots from his saddlebag while Nathaniel gathered an extra wrap. Their voices were barely a whisper.

"You should be safe tonight…." Nathaniel hesitated.

"James." His smile was nearly toothless. "My name is James."

"James." Nathaniel shook his outstretched hand. "Follow us."

The band returned the way they came, yet there were no tracks to follow. When they stopped at the edge of Daniel's field, the men smiled at their triumph. They slammed their rods together in celebration. Daniel widened his smile, for this is how he broke the tip off his rod last month.

The group split to their separate locations. Nathaniel and Daniel, together on one horse, and James on another made their way to Daniel's barn. Once inside, Daniel lifted a trap door in the floor. After quick instructions, James slid into the dark chamber and began to crawl through the hidden tunnel toward Daniel's home. With each progression he sidled closer to freedom.

Hanna checked her timepiece for the final time that evening. It was ten minutes to ten. She glared at her driver without uttering a sound. He squirmed on the buckboard seat in anticipation, yet he offered no excuse. He knew it would be moot.

"On your life, Joseph." She leaned into him. "Your life?" she mocked. "We shall see about that!"

His reddened face glowed as he turned the buckboard toward the Prenstrum farm.

Abigail smiled with relief when Nathaniel walked through the door. He shook the snow from his pants and started to relay the message of another successful quest. Excitement elevated his voice, and his hands moved through the air as he conveyed his story.

When he had stripped down to his last damp layer, he walked toward the hearth. It was then he noticed that she clutched bundles of cloth in her arms. Tears flooded his face. Abigail offered the wrapped baby to her husband and whispered through her tears, "She is Rebecca."

Nathaniel was hushed to silence by the guilt of his absence in the baby's birth. He took the bundle in his arms and gently kissed the baby's forehead. Rebecca's narrow fingers fumbled through his beard stubble. She winced and squirmed.

Nathaniel laughed, "Perhaps, I should shave for my little one." He turned his attention to his wife. His face was solemn. "She came early." He dropped his eyes and kissed the palm of Abigail's hand. "I'm sorry I was not near."

Abigail caressed his face. "All went well, though I would have to say, they gave me quite a scare."

Nathaniel was patient for her to continue. He swallowed hard. "They?"

"I had just brought in the last of the loose wood. When I sat in the fireside chair, the pain was intense. I knew it was time though it was too soon. I sent my wishes your way, but they would not break through."

Abigail continued without acknowledging his question. "I sat on the floor with my feet pressed against the hearth. The boiled water waited on the stove since early evening. I rested my back against the heavy chair and braced for the next wave of labor." Her sigh was heavy as she continued. "I was anxious when I saw feet coming first, but his movement was so swift I had no time to react." Abigail lowered her head and began to cry.

Nathaniel cradled them in his arms. This was not the news he was expecting. He stroked her long blonde hair as he whispered soft assurances to her.

"Shhh…it will be as planned. We will be fine."

Abigail's wet eyes met his. "He never took a breath." Her faint voice was barely heard above her cries, "It was my fault. I was uncertain of my actions…."

"That is not true, Abigail." He wrapped himself around her. "You have helped many women in childbirth." Nathaniel began ticking off the names, "Ruth Fluty…Vera Timmons…your own mother with the birth of your brother, John…Hanna Prens…." He stopped short. There was enough sadness in this house today.

He rocked Abigail in his arms until she fell limp. He kissed her gently and gathered the bundles from her arms. He lifted Abigail into the air and carried her to their bed. He covered her with an extra blanket and carried the babies into the sitting room.

He placed several logs on the fire and poked at the embers for a quick catch. The furniture chirped across the wooden floor as he rearranged their setting. The crib sat closest to the hearth. He placed Rebecca gently in the soft linens and held the other smaller thin bundle in his arms.

He opened the layers of soaked cloths until he stared at his son's face. He pulled the baby to his chest and began to cry. Rebecca quickly joined him.

After several unsuccessful attempts to quiet her, Nathaniel placed the wrapped bundle beside her. Immediately, she was calm. Tears dripped from Nathaniel's chin on his son's blanket. His face was tiny, sweet, and peaceful.

He spent the rest of the afternoon caring for Rebecca and Abigail. When the child cried and needed nurturing, he carried her to her mother. At times he allowed them to doze off together in each other's warmth. He thought it was the best medicine for Abigail's low spirit.

While they slept in the bedroom, he was busy in the sitting room. He carried a bed from the back bedroom and filled it with the warmest blankets he could find. He carried several loads of firewood in from the frigid air and filled the circular holder by the hearth.

After checking on his wife and child, he dressed in his now dry layers and went to the back yard. He walked to the barn with his ax in hand. A layer of sawdust fluttered in the air as he chased a chicken around the barn. He finally cornered it and snatched its neck. After one quick squawk its head was gone. The headless bird ran around the center of the barn until its final flop settled it against a pile of straw.

Nathaniel dipped the hen in boiling water, plucked the feathers, and gutted the bird. When he was finally satisfied with the beginnings of dinner, he placed the chicken in fresh water.

He hung the kettle on the fireplace crane and added a sliced onion and turnips. After counting the potatoes that remained in the crock, he decided tonight they would have to do without. He covered his body with his wool cloak and walked to the woodpile.

Abigail explained she had gathered all of the loose wood so he swung his bloody ax to free some logs. Wood splinters filled the air as he flung the firewood onto the ground. He spent nearly an hour filling the front porch. He placed the loose splinters for kindling in a wooden stave barrel near the door.

When his arms and back ached from the weight of the ax and wood, he undressed on the front porch and carried his wet clothes to the nails protruding from the barn beam mantle. He used Daniel's hand-wrought long-handled hook to swing the crane closer to him. The kettle swayed from the movement of the liquid within. He lifted the lid and drank in the smell of the simmering chicken. After adding salt, he walked to the bedroom.

The air in the room was noticeably colder than the small sitting room. Rebecca was suckling quietly. Her hands fluttered through the thin air. Through red-rimmed, down-turned eyes, Abigail smiled.

Nathaniel leaned against the poplar doorframe. He made no mention of his son.

"I have the sitting room prepared for us. Its warmth will be welcomed." He hesitated, "When you are ready."

"I am ready. I feel my milk will not spoil for it is half-frozen," she managed a soft chortle.

The three spent the evening in the comfort of the blazing fire. With her stomach full of chicken stew, Abigail settled between the blankets. The bed that Nathaniel made was comfortable, yet sleep eluded her.

Normally the low murmur of her husband's snore lulled her to slumber but not this night. She laid her hand on her daughter and felt for warmth and movement. She held the child much of the night, nudging gently as a reminder to breathe. Her face was drawn by the day's first light.

She chastised herself for not preparing her body for nursing. Her soft tissue cracked and bled. The achievement should have been pleasurable, but for Abigail it held much pain. She knew it would get better with time. Her skin would toughen and be prepared for teething, but at the moment she was faced with many weeks of suffering.

The balance of the winter found the Kristol family spending their time between the sitting room, kitchen, and barn. Nathaniel cooked the meals for nearly a week before Abigail insisted control.

"You do not settle it in the normal way," she scolded.

Truth be told, he wanted to surrender the meals and laundry back to her. He imagined his mother chasing him out of her kitchen — a wooden spoon held high in her hand as he burst through the door, clutching a sliver of pumpkin pie.

"What brings such joy to your face, Nathaniel?"

His grin grew wider, "Thoughts of mother and her *own* stove. Her feelings did not differ much from yours," he laughed.

"Go on now, before I gather my spoon!"

Nathaniel's belly laugh continued until the barn door closed behind him. Abigail finished her daily chores. Her silent tears helped to salt the water.

3

"Wake up. Wake up. *Wake up!*" came the whispered plea in Abigail's ears. She moved in her startled slumber listening for the sound of her husband's voice again. Only his snores were heard.

She threw the blankets from her body. The heavy grey wool held to her feet in denial. She tumbled to the floor in a thud. The sharp pain in her ankle left little doubt.

With the remnants of '*Wake up*' echoing through her, she pulled her body to Rebecca's crib. In the soft moonlight she listened for the low breath of her baby. She heard none.

The child's face was blue. She lifted Rebecca quickly from her cradle and slapped her back. The cry of her daughter never sounded so sweet. She nestled the child in her arms and cried. Nathaniel's snoring ceased as he rolled over onto his side. His face was hidden from view.

"Shhh, my little one. I have you."

She positioned herself in the hickory rocker that Nathaniel had made for her this past Christmas. Her foot and leg throbbed. She elevated her leg on the brick hearth. She was relieved that she could wiggle her toes.

"Just a sprain," she whispered.

The sound of her baby's breaths comforted her. She pushed her ankle's pain from her thoughts and focused on the whispered alarm telling her to wake up. She felt a chill slither down her back and grinned at the feeling of the thin hairs on her arm rising.

She whispered to her daughter, "I heard the voice of your angel." She moved her mouth close to Rebecca's infant ear. "It's a man."

Shuffling feet at the funeral door startled her. She held her breath to listen. The familiar scrape punctuated by a thud at the side entrance could only represent one theme — another slave would arrive by train. She listened as the muffled sound of a single rider rode through the snow.

Nathaniel rose from their warm bed to address the visitor. He walked across the hall into the library or gentleman's room that was across the center hall from the sitting room. A pair of double doors closed the conversations from moving through the house, for this room held much secrecy.

The funeral door was a narrow door on the south side of the house. It opened into the library. Its threshold was built to buggy height, and during dreadful weather it was the door through which most women entered. It allowed them ease of movement into the house without touching the ground. Its main purpose, however, was for which it was named — funerals. Only twenty-nine inches in width, the opening allowed barely an inch of clearance for the sides of the casket to pass through.

The double doors into the center hall were opened to allow the guests to visit the mourned. When the viewing was over, the casket was taken out the funeral door and slid into the back of a buckboard. The flowers, which adorned the front of the house signifying an interment, were gathered and placed onto the wagon. All were taken to the cemetery and left as a gift of remembrance.

Nathaniel opened the double doors. The air was brisk in the unfrequented room. He shuffled across the poplar floor. The opening crack of the lock echoed through the house. The wind rushed through the hall as an announcement of intentions. Flapping in the wind were the edges of a piece of paper secured by an iron rod. He pulled both items through the door.

Abigail covered Rebecca from the blast of the bitter February air. She watched as Nathaniel walked through the room muttering the numbers written on the paper. She made no mention of her swelling ankle.

He reappeared dressed for a day's ride. He kissed Abigail and Rebecca and walked to the barn. He saddled Kit quickly and gathered several rods that stood in the corner of an empty stall.

The iron rod had several purposes, but its main function served as a silent call to freedom when placed at the side door of each abolitionist's home. The rod left in the early morning signified a slave would be traveling on the first morning train. If it appeared at mid-day, the smuggled slave would be hidden on the noon train; and if the rod were found in the evening, the slave would be found at the nine-thirty stop.

Most of the slaves were placed secretively inside a cattle car. When the door was closed, a lock secured it. Those railcars had to be protected from many types of bandits – slave smugglers, cattle thieves, and the malicious Copperheads.

Although the stop at Salem hosted several daily trains, only three held smuggled slaves. The one constant was the same group of men in charge to refuel, replenish, and protect the cargo while the engine halted. One major flaw, which made guarding this stop difficult, was the aggressive bend at the station. Only the first ten railcars' opposing sides were visible from the platform. Most of the year this deficit did not affect the watchful eyes of the sentinel, but in the winter with the snow piled high, guarding against the culprits was nearly impossible.

Nathaniel placed his final rod against Daniel's door before the ten o'clock hour was finished. His ride had taken him over eight miles. His face felt frozen to the touch, and he could not remember the last time he had feeling in his fingers. The only warmth he felt was from Kit.

By the time his footsteps hit the front porch, Abigail had finished heating the remnants of yesterday's rabbit stew. She pulled apart some over-dried bits of bread and lined two bowls with their pieces. She placed the steaming bowls on the fireside table.

"All go as planned?" she asked.

Nathaniel grunted in reply. He was too focused on rubbing his rigid fingers over the rising vapor. Finally, he answered, "Yes. There will be six attending."

Abigail knew not to ask many questions. It was not the place of the woman to know. This was man's business — grave business. The group felt it be best for their wives to know little in the case of Copperhead interrogations.

It had only happened once. Her name was Dorothy Nerale. She was the wife of Abigail's first cousin, Jacob. She was recovering from the difficult birth of her fourth child. She had birthed twins only eleven months prior and this fourth child was born with impatience.

Abigail had helped with her delivery and stayed with her for the following four days. They were difficult, but Dorothy began to show signs of improvement. On the fifth day Abigail began her trip toward home. It was a two-day ride.

When she opened the front door, the house was empty. A single metal rod was placed against the gathering table. It only meant one thing.

When Nathaniel arrived safely, his face was grave. He explained their unexpected ordeal.

"We arrived at the station as planned and waited for the train's arrival. Just before the whistle sounded, three unknown men joined us. We accepted our fate as sure death, but when the men fully revealed themselves, they also held freedom rods. We let our guard down. We were wrong."

He hung his head and explained the series of events. Abigail's eyes held terror as he continued his tale of defeat and gore.

He sighed, "At last, they pulled the slaves from their knees and disappeared into the darkness." He clenched his fists. "I fear the worst."

Abigail sighed at her husband's remorse. After a long pause she whispered, "How were you known?"

Nathaniel held her hand. "It was through Dorothy's words they found us. They were her last."

Hanna Prenstrum was a secret leader of the Copperheads. She came from the South and held the view that no Negro slave should be free. They were purchased property, no different than land or animals. Their purpose was to work the land, the farm, whatever needed tending — without words or any trouble.

Her sister, Camellia Ward, lived on a twelve hundred acre plantation in Georgia. She owned more than 200 slaves and paid top auction price for many of them. She had their slave chains made from a heavier metal than most. Connected to each neck chain was a round tag. The front of the marker was engraved with the Ward family crest; on the back was only the slave's first name unless Camellia could not pronounce it. Then they were given a good Christian name. The links of the chain were custom-fitted around the slave's neck. "Perfectly snug," her words were repeated. "For their safety," she always added. When completed, only the tag had movement.

Most of the purchased slaves accepted this outward show of ownership with grace; only a few resisted. If

Camellia or her husband, Samuel, found them without their marker, it was fitted one link tighter the second time; God forbid there be a third.

Many of the normal Southern crops grew on their plantation — cotton, peaches, okra — but theirs also boasted some of the best peanuts in the state. The rich soil yielded an abundant crop for which the Wards received handsome payment.

They had a few trusted black men that they used as overseers. The men had a genuine rapport with their assigned groups. Only one man seemed to constantly call attention to himself. His name was George — only George. He had been without his last name for so long that even he could not recall it. He was on his second set of chain reductions. Most of his peers would have shown him sympathy, but he brought it on his own they whispered.

He was taken from Africa when he was only seven. A group of armed men ambushed George and his father while tilling a field. They were beaten, bound, and forced to march from their land. His only recollection of his mother was her scream as they were torn from the village, yet his memories of her face were long lost.

They were driven hard for two days until their feet met the ocean shore. The dock's wood planks were slippery with blood. Free natives hid their faces from the armed guards as they tossed rotten Kei apples toward the ship. George's nostrils burned from the foul smell. He slipped on the putrid yellow flesh and nearly plunged into the angry ocean. The dock master's fingers snatched his neck chain and pulled him from a sure drowning. A sharp slap on his back signaled silence. He shuffled to the dock's end and fell on the deck of the ship.

Gathered to his feet by his shirt, he struggled to keep his breath. He was ushered quickly to a lower level. The room was dark and crowded. His body was the last thrown into the mob. A sharp metal object broke his fall and tore at the flesh above his right eye. He could feel his face swell as the warm blood spilled over his chin. The moisture gathered onto his shirt and stiffened as it dried. He dared not make a sound. His eyes searched the darkened space for his father, but he could not be found.

The seas were rough, and the group huddled together for safety. Many evaded their emotions, their eyes hollow from forgotten hope, and others lost their stomachs in disbelief. Silence was their common bond.

George landed on the southern shores of Georgia in 1837. He was a rather husky child of seven, and the auctioneer touted him as a lad of nine. His birthday was listed as the following month, which would make him appear to be turning ten. That age brought considerably more money. When the Wards purchased him that sweltering day in August, they thought they were buying a more mature child, one that understood the ways of the South and of slavery. They could not have been more wrong.

George spent many evening hours hiding in the bushes imitating the girls of the manor as they traced their works of art with a lead pencil. He mimicked how they made their frail hands move over the paper.

Once he held his own pencil and drew lines on the white paper. He gasped at the wonder. The stick made very dark marks. He moved his hands over the lead to erase it and fell to disappointment when it smeared. The faster his hands rubbed the paper, the worse the smudge.

The girls giggled and Camellia heard them. She was shocked when she opened the door to find George sitting there with her precious little ones. The Ward sisters claimed innocence, and George was pulled from the cushioned chair. He slid the pencil into his pants. That first beating left a dark mark in his memory.

When his battered body was thrown onto the dirt floor, the slave women rushed to care for him. His split, swollen lips tried to smile as he pulled the pencil from the waistband of his pants and straightened a piece of crumpled parchment damp with his own sweat. He amazed his peers by pretending to read an elaborate story. Only his eyes fell on the grey blotches smeared over the surface of the paper. The group of listeners held their breath until he finished. He quietly folded the parchment, smiled, and spit out the first of many bloody teeth.

His desire to learn to read and write could not be quenched. He watched the girls from the shadows as the months turned into years. Occasionally, he was invited to join them, and as time went on he began to learn.

His pretend written stories were wild and full of imagination. At times, the entire slave house swelled with such laughter that it caused attention from the manor house. When Master Ward opened the door, the slaves parted wide for easy access to George. He was pulled from the crowd by his chain collar and was not seen for days. They could easily 'set him in his place' when he was younger, but by the time George turned fifteen he was better prepared for his escape.

It happened in September. George sat on his hindquarters over the lumbering kettle fire. He stoked the last of its embers at midnight. He stared at the amber light framed by the manor house windows until all went dark. As the final piece of evidence that he existed on this earth, he picked up a stick and swirled his name in the sandy soil beside the fire. The bold juvenile letters — GORGᴲ — were unmistakable.

He gathered his rolled blanket secured by a leather strap and flung it over his shoulder. A tin cup and makeshift water jug hung from the end of a knot. A small drawn bag held a few pieces of flint and magnesium for fire making. His grey linen knickers hung free around his shins, and the knife blade tucked into his waist tightened his pants just enough to keep them from slipping off his hips. He wore no shoes. He didn't own any.

George walked in the opposite direction of the manor. He felt comfortable to follow the road under the cover of darkness. On occasion, he heard horses as they galloped closer, and he hid in the thicket until long after they had passed. He traveled many miles in complete silence.

He slept during the day in the brush out of sight of the road, yet near enough to hear the day's travelers. His leather hat kept the rain from his eyes and the sun from his cheeks. After the fourth day he had worked one of the links loose enough to pull his slave chain from his neck. It had been tightly fastened for so long that his skin grew over a few links. He uttered not a sound when he pulled the chain and flesh from his neck. He stared at the bloody marker as it lay on the ground. He felt free for the first time in his life. He knelt to gather the chain. His head hit the ground with a thud.

George woke to the imprisonment of full body chains as he thrashed in an open buckboard. The metal collar that surrounded his neck had two chains attached that led to his wrists; two more chains extended to ankle bracelets. It was impossible to lie straight or to stand erect with the shortened length. It was most difficult to try to walk but try he must — all the way through the front door of his master's house.

When they pulled the black cloth from his face, his eyes fell on Camellia. She screamed so many words he could not discern one. She shook her finger in his down-turned face and slapped his cheeks until the tingling stopped. Her husband pulled him from the porch by the lead chain. He struggled to keep his balance and was dragged until he found his feet. Anger drove Master Ward to do what he did next, and George did his best to try to forget it. He tried to remember the day in the woods. He remembered seeing his slave marker attached to his chain on the ground. He fought the urge to spit on it, and then all went black.

He cursed himself for not being more aware. He tried to remember if he felt watched, or hunted, yet he denied both. He felt safe, free, and alone until he woke in the wagon.

His head suffered so many wounds from his beating that it was difficult to locate the original blow. His body ached as his wounds pounded from infection. With swollen, blistered lips he longed for a drink, yet there was one thing he desired more — freedom. His pride suffered. His hopes were crushed, yet he dreamed of trying again.

5

By the spring of 1854, George had long settled at Oak Bend. He no longer wrestled with his slave tag and its consistent choking. His dreams of freedom were pushed aside, and the Wards rewarded his loyalty by branding him an overseer. At aged twenty-four, he watched many repeat offenders slain or beaten to death for attempted escapes and remembered his past actions with shame.

Master Ward was a frugal man and never desired to take the life of his possessions unless absolutely necessary. There were only a few in that category, and no one ever forgot them.

Their graves were on the north end of the plantation, far from view of the manor. Shredded straw mixed with the red Georgia dirt was packed into a form that had been chiseled out of a large boulder by the graveyard. When the mixture met with the right consistency, it was pounded into the rock's hand-fashioned void. Songs of the gathered voices lifted through the air muffled only by their tears.

It was always George who carved the name into the clay mold. As the sun heated the rock, the marker dried to perfection. It was carefully removed and placed at the head of the dead. George was present for the eighth one buried in that place. There were now twenty-eight markers.

It had been years since the first time George was pulled from the front porch. The Ward sisters were now grown, married, and lived on their own plantations. They each had three children — all girls.

The youngest granddaughter, Lacey, took a special liking to George. They had many quick visits on the porch until Camellia shooed him away. Lacey's fair hair and waving hand were visible from George's shack. When his feet shuffled through his front door, he returned the gesture. Only then did Lacey stop. She refused to acknowledge her grandmother's warnings about "taking up with the slaves."

By Lacey's seventh birthday, she met with George regularly. She supplied him with his own pencil and as many bits of paper she could find. Many she retrieved from the trash.

She taught George how to spell and form his letters correctly, facing each letter in the proper direction. He had the most trouble with the letter E. No matter how he tried to convince himself, it still looked better to his eyes facing left. Lacey's blue eyes trimmed in awning-like eyelashes convinced him she was right. It was her mother, Lilly, who taught him wrong.

"George," Lacey repeated, "this is the *right* way." She placed her lily-white hand over his dark, leathery skin and helped move his hand until the perfect letter E was finished. "Now, do it by yourself."

"But it goes better this way." George drew it backwards.

Lacey's eyes never left her paper. "No. That is incorrect. Do it again."

George drew an E. She looked at it, shook her head, and smirked, "Again."

Before long George accomplished full sentences and could read most of Lacey's materials. She tore pages from the church songbook, stole papers from her grandfather's desk, and even brought hand-written letters. George did well but had a difficult time reading the scrolled pen and ink. Yet, Lacey made him try.

"This is how people write. You are going to have to learn it."

"Yes, Miss. I'll try, but…"

"No buts, you *will* learn." Her attitude was infectious.

Lacey's visits became less frequent the following three years. She attended charm and stitching school and only saw George once a month.

In February of 1857 the weather turned unseasonably warm. Lacey had not visited the plantation since late October. George feared to ask Lady Ward of Lacey's news, so he relied on the housemaids and the cook to supply him with word.

Lacey ailed from a rare blood disease, and her health continued to decline despite the doctor's efforts. Repeatedly, she begged her mother to visit Oak Bend, but her mother would not permit it. Finally, after a brief sign of improvement, her request to return to the plantation was granted.

When she arrived at Grandma Camellia's, her carpetbag and corset were stuffed with letters, wanted posters, and papers. She had been saving many things for George, but this time she had something special.

George watched Lacey ride her pony around the track as she often did. Her mother talked softly with Camellia as George approached.

He tipped his hat, "Ma'am."

Lilly wiped her eyes, "George."

The three stood in silence as Lacey bounced around the track. Her opulent smile met his, yet from the distance, the sickness around her eyes was clearly visible. A lone tear slid down his cheek.

Camellia's stern response cast a shadow across his face. "This will be her last visit, George. Be certain it is pleasant." She clicked her button-up heels together and turned from both of them.

George shuddered at Camellia's comment confident their visits were secret. He felt safe, secure, and alone; just as he deemed on his attempted escape years before. He was stunned into silence. He chastised his thoughts for trusting his instincts.

Lilly laid her hand on his shoulder. Tears moistened her cheeks. "Lacey does not know. She also thinks your discussions are a secret. It's best we leave it that way." Her eyes begged for confirmation.

George hung his head. "Yes, Ma'am."

His thoughts raced through their meetings. He remembered the first time Lacey rode to the graveyard. They had just pulled Percy's marker from the stone. All eyes rested on this little girl who respected their reverence. She slid from her pony, clutching a field daisy. In silence she placed it on the fresh mound of dirt, closed her eyes, and whispered a prayer. Not a slave moved — not a sound was heard. All held their breath.

George was the only one to speak, "Thank you, Miss."

"You are welcome," came in a singsong reply.

The group watched in disbelief as she rode out of sight. They murmured among themselves.

"George, you brought this on us." George looked at them in disbelief.

One to his left whispered, "If we get caught, the price will be heavy."

"It will be your head," said another.

"You shouldn't hold up with the Master's kin."

"It's trouble I tell you…trouble!"

Shouts erupted. Above the wails a young man's voice bellowed. His eyes were wide as his voice rattled. "There aren't `nuf spaces for all of us!"

The crowd murmurs settled to a hush. Their eyes moved over those standing and imagined their bodies buried in the ground. The statement was true. The graveyard was too small.

In the distance a band of horses appeared over the knoll. The little blonde girl rode among them. The slaves screamed and scattered. Only George remained.

They pulled his body from the cemetery in silence. He did not resist; the attempt would be futile. He permitted his mind to wander to places beyond — land that was free and his, without worry or fear. With each strike of the barbed whip, his misty eyes moved further into the distant fields of imagined freedom. The scent of white lilies filled the air. His feet floated over the freshly-mown grass. His mind protected him from his most brutal and final beating.

When they tossed his broken body into the hot box in the yard, his vision of freedom went dark. For three days he lay without bread and water until Lacey brought relief. Had it not been for her compassion he would have met certain death. There in the yard, with a layer of metal between them, Lacey and George's bond became unbreakable.

The sound of Lilly's voice returned his thoughts to the present. She managed a thin smile.

"I had Lacey followed each time she left the house. The guard was told to never intervene unless needed." A puff of dust left his shirt as she patted his arm. "I knew she was teaching you, George. We *all* knew."

She threw her head in the air and laughed. It felt good to expel the energy. Too many of her days were consumed with sadness.

"George, I have a confession. Do you know what *confession* means?"

"Yes, Ma'am."

"My sister and I taught you to write your name with only one E and it was backwards." George tilted his head in confusion. "We knew that if you ever tried to escape again, that was one way you could be identified." The smile slid from her face. "I am ashamed, George. You have never shown anything but kindness toward my daughter and me, and we repay you with continued cruelty."

Tears blanketed her words. She hung her head.

"Lacey and I have begged Mother and Father for your freedom. It was not until Lacey became ill that I knew what I had to do, but…." She grabbed George's arm in desperation. "You must not tell a soul. This betrayal would kill my father."

"I don't understand, Ma'am."

Lilly turned to see Camellia return with a tray of ginger iced tea. The tray held three glasses.

"Not a word to anyone. You must promise." Her voice was reduced to a whisper. "Lacey will explain. Promise me, George. Say it."

"Ye…Yes, Ma'am. I promise."

Lilly wiped the tears from her eyes and held her breath as she waited for her mother to re-join them. Camellia waved to Lacey to join them. She gave the chilled glasses to Lacey and Lilly and gathered the last one for herself.

It would have never occurred to Camellia to extend the courtesy to George, nor would he have expected it. Camellia drank the chilled tea until it was empty. Lilly took one sip and held the glass in guilt. Lacey brought the glass to her lips but did not take a drink. She lifted the glass in the air and extended it to George.

His eyes were frozen wide. Lacey giggled at the expression on his face.

"George, it is hot. Take a drink." She jingled the ice in the glass.

Camellia began to speak in protest, but Lilly silenced her with her eyes and a tight squeeze of her wrist.

George waited for approval from Lilly. She nodded to him as a gesture of acceptance. He smiled at Lacey.

"Hurry, George. The ice is going to melt," Lacey teased.

He took the glass from her frail hand. It felt cool and heavy. He brought it to his mouth and took a sip. He closed his lips on the glass rim. It was the first time he had drawn a drink from something other than his hand or a tin cup.

Lacey giggled. "Drink it all, George. Drink it all."

He lifted the glass to his lips again. It felt cool on his bare gums. The ice cubes slipped into his mouth and rattled against the only two teeth he had left. The look of surprise on his face made Camellia smile though she quickly dismissed it.

He drank the contents and held the last ice cube in his mouth until it melted. "Thank you, Ma'am."

Camellia held the empty tray before him. Without a word, he took it from her, placed his glass on it, gathered the other two, and carried it to the house. He watched from the front porch as Lacey danced with excitement; her body doubled with laughter.

ebruary's storm halted the arrival of spring in the year of Rebecca's birth. The snow continued to build and refused to recede until late April. Finally, the green tips of the daffodils pushed through the heavy white blanket. By the end of May, their yellow faces faded to brown from the heat of the early summer sun.

The newborn had a voracious appetite, and within a few months Rebecca showed no lingering signs of being a premature baby. Her chubby face was filled with brightness and a constant smile. She was a quiet, reflective child.

The years passed quickly. Rebecca grew to her youth without any siblings. She spent many hours sitting on the ground behind the barn where her brother was buried. A carved wooden cross marked his grave.

From the clothesline, Abigail watched her daughter chatter to the monument. Rebecca's hands busily groomed the flowers and pulled the weeds while she included her brother in the day's events. The tilt of her head and sudden burst of laughter spurred Abigail's tears. She hid her face in the swaying laundry.

Nathaniel's involvement in the Abolitionist Movement kept him away from home on many evenings. The secret meetings in the glen became more frequent and taxing, though the reward of a slave's freedom proved worthy.

During Nathaniel's absence, Abigail and Rebecca busied their hands with fabric and needles. Rebecca's nimble fingers grew quite skilled with her tiny, tight stitches. Before long she completed her first lap quilt.

The only talent that paled to her stitching was the printed word. She spent hours reading aloud to her mother. Whether she read the Bible, the Bugle, or a letter, tenacity was her best friend. Rarely did she ask her mother for help. By Rebecca's eighth birthday neither Nathaniel nor Abigail read the newspaper silently. Their daughter's fluent speech became a joy to their ears as it fueled Rebecca's fire to help the oppressed. Soon, she would ask to join the cause.

George walked to the cemetery in deep thought. He was puzzled by the conversation he had with Lilly. He wondered about his special present from Lacey. He turned to look toward the direction of the manor. From over a distant knoll he saw Lacey's hair bouncing about her. Her colt, running with grace and speed, carried her faithfully along an unmarked path.

Lacey's wide smile greeted George as she broke through the bowing limbs of the live oak trees. She slid from her pony and pulled a large bundle from the saddlebag. She walked to the grave marker boulder and motioned for George to join her.

In silence George sat beside his frail friend. He swallowed hard to remove the gathering lump of sadness that threatened to steal his breath. His watery eyes met hers.

"Why the sadness?" she asked with youthful innocence.

George wanted to blurt out his feelings. He wanted to explain how much he would miss her, how grateful he was that she spent time teaching him, and how honored he was to call her his friend. He lifted his shoulders and shrugged instead.

Lacey started to open a few of the papers. She separated them on the surface of the flat rock and held them in place with stones that George automatically gathered on his walk. She explained each pile's significance.

"Now, this one is some of Mother's new music." She ran her fingers over the surface of one. "I've been learning to play this one, but I think it would be best for you to have it because the words are important ones." She handed it to George. "Read it to me."

George's trembling hands took the single sheet of music from Lacey's thin fingers.

He read the words deliberately masking his brokenness. When he finished all four verses, Lacey clapped her hands in triumph.

"George, that was wonderful. You are doing very well." She pointed to the word *salvation* and giggled, "Even this one was perfect!"

She rummaged through the next pile and pulled out a torn section of printed hemp. The ink was bold, black, and somewhat smeared. It showed signs of water damage and Lacey did her best to preserve what was written.

"Now read this one."

George moved the paper closer to his face and then pulled it farther away. He crinkled his nose at Lacey. She smiled.

"Just try. You can do it."

"But the words are smeared."

"George, you have to learn how to read everything. The words are not always going to be perfect." She moved her hand beside her mouth and lowered her voice. "Sometimes it is *this* writing that is the most important."

George did his best to read what was before him. He struggled with many words, and Lacey helped him sound them out. After several attempts he finished the document.

"Now comes the hard part," Lacey stated without emotion. "Tell me in your own words what you just read."

"Well," George started, "It seems to be an...invat...invata...."

"Invitation."

"Yeah, invitation to a...party."

"No, not a party, something else." Lacey watched George crinkled his nose again. "Read it again, faster this time. Maybe that will help."

He read it again. He hesitated over the words *commence*, *movement*, and *abolitionist*, but the one that stuck in his mouth and refused to come out was *slavery*.

He knew the word well. He knew the feeling. He lived the life. He knew the beatings. And he knew the desire to be free from it, but he could not say it.

"Say it, George."

"I can't Miss Lacey. It's too hard."

"Why?"

"Because it is."

"I do not understand. What's hard?"

"Everythin'."

"Everything? Or just that word?"

"Not the word, the thing."

"What thing?"

George slammed his heavy fist over the bold letters – SLAVERY. "This thing." The tip of his broad finger covered the majority of the print and worked hard to erase it from the paper.

Lacey huffed in disgust. "That thing," she gently removed his finger and tapped the same word, "has a way

38

of jumping off the paper and out of your mouth. You have to say it."

"I can't."

"Can't or won't?"

"Won't."

"You are a very stubborn man, George." Lacey crossed her arms in front of her.

"Please sound out the word for me."

He shook his head no.

"Why?"

"Cuz you don't see it, that's why." George spit his words in frustration.

Lacey understood what he meant, and he was right. Even as a young child she knew how wrong slavery was. She loved her grandparents but did not understand their lack of compassion for the abuse.

Lacey remembered her secret visits to George when he was imprisoned in the hot box. Many times she smuggled bread and water to him. Twice she brought a chunk of ice wrapped in a cloth and recalled wiping the tears from her face when he returned the cloth soaked with blood. She picked Lady's Mantle to wrap his sores and gave him fresh strips of cloth to cover them from infection. In fear of discovery she buried the discarded dressing.

She watched in horror from the veranda as her grandfather pulled George from the box, beat his back with a leather strap, and tossed him through the doorframe of his shack. Grandpa's hateful words still rang in her ears, and she could not shake the guilt.

"It was my fault, you know," she finally whispered in remorse.

"'Twas no one's fault, Miss Lacey...no one's fault."

The two sat in silence for several minutes. Lacey's fingers subconsciously traced the edges of the hole carved into the rock. Her voice cracked.

"Did you do this?"

"Yep."

She pointed to the many hand-made markers before them, "For them?"

"Yep." George felt the lump growing again.

Pools flooded her wide eyes. "Why is there slavery, George?"

His mouth hung open but not a sound left. He had never been asked that question before from a slave, let alone the granddaughter of his master. Again, he shrugged his shoulders.

"If you didn't live at Oak Bend, then where?"

That was another question that he did not know how to answer. He wanted to shout *'Anywhere but here,'* but that wasn't entirely true. He enjoyed the people in his band. He was well fed, had a dry place to lay his head, and even had fresh water to drink. The day's labor was long and hard, but that usually was cause for a peaceful night's sleep. He enjoyed the responsibility Master Ward and Lady Camellia had given to him, especially after the way their relationship began, but what he enjoyed most were these visits with Lacey. A smile covered his face.

"George, you are smiling."

"I'm happy, Miss Lacey."

Continuing the vein, Lacey questioned, "Happy to be a slave?"

He coughed at the words and choked back the tears. "No, Miss Lacey. I'm not happy to be a slave. I'm happy to be sittin' here with you."

She patted his leathery skin and smiled back at him. The grin lasted for barely a second. Her face twisted from pain, and she fell limp in George's arms.

He stood in a panic. He felt her neck for a pulse. It was weak but present. His thick fingers gently patted her cheek until her eyes finally opened. She faded in and out of consciousness for several minutes. Their sporadic conversation continued.

Lacey lay in George's arms. Her eyes were closed as tears of pain flowed from them.

She spoke in whispers. "Tell me about the grave markers, George."

He told Lacey about how he carved the outline of the marker in the rock. He explained how to mix the mud and line the form with straw. His voice was full of pride when he explained that only he could write, and it was his job to scribe the name of the dead into the wet mixture.

Lacey listened intently and asked only a few questions. She was comforted by the sound of his voice and the strength of his arms.

When George finished his story, Lacey grew restless. She wiggled free of his arms and forced herself to sit upright. Her trembling finger pointed to the damned word.

"Say it for me, George. *Please* say it for me."

George crinkled his nose and forced his eyes closed. He moved his lips to form the word but could not force the sound to go with it.

"Please, George. It's important to me."

"Why, Miss Lacey? Why?"

"Just say it."

After a minute of silence, the word was pushed from his lips, "Slavery." He hung his head in submission.

"Now say *Free*."

George tossed a puzzled look to his frail teacher. His mouth held a half-grin. "Free," he said with ease.

"Good. Now repeat after me."

"I, George…."

"I, George," he mocked

Lacey continued through his sarcasm. "Am free from slavery."

His face softened from the sound of those sweet words. "What do you mean, Miss Lacey?"

"It's just an exercise, George. Something someday you will need to say."

He smiled at her innocent game and repeated, "…Am free from slavery."

She closed her eyes and asked him to repeat it. After ten times they erupted into laughter.

Lacey gathered her legs under her and stood. Her vision narrowed and she nearly crumpled to the ground twice before George picked her up. He carried Lacey to her colt and placed her on the saddle.

With the grace of a grown woman, though barely aged ten, she whispered, "I will never forget you, George. And please do not forget those words." A thin smile graced her lips.

His eyes flooded with tears choking his reply. He watched her body slump forward as she wrapped her arms around the colt's neck. The last image George had of Lacey was her ritual wave of goodbye as she disappeared from his view. He collapsed to the ground and sobbed.

It was four-thirty on a Sunday morning. George woke to a hoarse call of his name accompanied by a quick rap on his door.

"George!" she whispered. As soon as he saw the housemaid's face, he understood the news. "Miss Lacey...Miss Lacey's gone to be wif the Lord."

George held onto the doorframe for strength as she relayed the message. He made no attempt to wipe the tears from his cheeks. They sprinkled his shirt until it was soaked.

"Miss Lilly is comin' to see you today. Yes suh, comin' to see you. Says she's got somethin' for yas. From Miss Lacey. Boss don't know nothin' 'bout it. Yes suh...a secret. A secret for George." She hummed a tune to herself as she shuffled back to the manor kitchen.

George watched her body sway to the tune. Grief blurred his vision. He wiped his nose onto his sleeve and whispered Lacey's name to the sky. His life would never be the same.

The daily mundane chores did not hold George's attention. He stared toward the manor more often than tilling the vegetable beds. His band worked harder to make up for his lack of attention.

When the carriage finally arrived, the driver helped Lilly and her mother with their bags. Master Ward met the women with open arms. Their cries were heard throughout the plantation. From a far distance George joined their sighs. The world had lost a very special little girl.

By dusk George had given up hope of Lilly's visit. He dragged his blistered feet into his dingy house and knelt on the floor beside his straw bed. His hands fumbled for the hidden bundle and pulled it out of its hiding place. Cross-legged on the floor, he began to untie the rope that bound the package. He swallowed the growing lump in his throat. In his hands was a grave marker. His own hand did the writing. He permitted the tears to come. They wet the name *Lacey*. He held it to his chest.

A soft knock on his door startled him. He wiped his face quickly and called out to his visitor.

"Leave me be."

"George. It's Lilly."

He scrambled to his feet and lunged at the door. His face was flushed as the door hung limp on its hinges. Lilly stood in the opening speechless and drawn from months of sorrow. She threw her arms around him and sobbed until her tears were gone. George stood with one hand around her; the other held Lacey's marker.

"Oh, George," she finally sobbed. "How can we live without our Miss Lacey?"

They sat together for a long time on the front step of his shack. Lilly explained every detail of the past months. She laughed and cried as she shared her daughter's bravery in facing her disease. When she had finished speaking, she uncovered a wooden box. She placed it in George's hands.

"This is a gift from Lacey. She made me promise to give this to you in secret."

George picked up the box in the dim light and tried to open the lid.

"It's locked." She laughed. "That is most curious of all. Lacey gave me all of the instructions but did not give me the key. I thought, perhaps, it was another well-hidden secret from the pair of you."

George never lifted his eyes, "No, Ma'am."

Lilly stared into his soft brown eyes and smiled. "I decided that if anyone was going to break the lock, it would have to be the person for whom the contents were intended. It was not up to me to break that confidence."

George lowered his head from discovery. "Thank you, Ma'am."

"Do you know what is in here, George?"

"No, Ma'am. I reckon it's more readin' papers. Lacey said she would send more."

"She was always a girl of her word." She sniffed back the tears, stiffened her shoulders, stood, and straightened her dress. Her posture screamed a proud Southern lady.

"I must be going before I am missed." She wrapped her arms around George one last time. Her words came in a hushed voice, "Lacey loved you, George."

With tears streaming silently down his face he whispered, "I felt the same way, Ma'am. Sure 'nuf the same way."

Lilly stepped into the darkness. The soft swish of her dress in the dewy grass moved farther from him until it suddenly stopped.

"George!" came a hushed voice.

"Yes, Ma'am?" He moved toward Lilly's voice.

"I forgot to tell you. Lacey's last words were…'Tell George to remember. Tell him to remember.' What does that mean, George?"

"Ma'am?" Her eyes studied him until she picked up her dress and walked toward the house.

George carried his precious package and closed the door behind him. He fumbled for the rawhide string that hung around his neck. Knotted at the end was a tiny silver key that Lacey had given him on her last visit. He placed the key in the lock, but it didn't open. After several unsuccessful tries, he broke the lock open with a chisel.

Neatly placed inside the box were several piles of papers. On top was a note written by Lacey explaining their purpose: some for music, some for reading, and sections of a newspaper for news of the outside world. George was fascinated with the newspaper. He had heard about the printed word but had never held one. He read its pages with little difficulty.

On the bottom of the box was a white handkerchief. It was embroidered with the initials LWT. He cried for Lacey one more time as he brought her linen to his nose. It held a faint scent of white lilies.

As George began to place his special treasures back in the box, he noticed a keyhole. He fumbled again for the key on the string. The lock sprung open with ease.

Gingerly, he lifted the false bottom of the box. Four items were placed in this space — a folded piece of parchment paper, a gold pocket watch, a small brown pouch, and a complete newspaper titled The Anti-Slavery Bugle from Salem, Ohio.

George opened the letter from Lacey first. It read:

What are the words, George? Say them to me now – loud enough for me to hear. In this box you will find four things.

First, this note. Destroy it after you have read it. Do not keep it. It may cause you harm.

Second is the newspaper. You will need The Bugle for your trip. I have circled and numbered three names. These men are your contacts in that order. Memorize their names and their towns, George. Do not forget them.

Third is the pouch of coins. It's not much, but it will help. Guard it well and keep it hidden.

The final item is a pocket watch. You will need to be timely. It's important.

One last time for me, say the words.

George choked as he whispered, "I, George, am free from slavery." His tears blurred her note. He crumpled it and tossed it into his outside fire.

Rebecca twirled in her new calico dress until she was dizzy. Her mother laughed at her nine-year-old innocence until she could no longer catch her breath. Rebecca crumpled to the floor with her head swooning and eyes unable to focus.

With her spinning world slowing down to normalcy, she became quiet. She stared out of the kitchen window as her father approached on his horse. She jumped to her feet and ran barefoot out the door.

"Daddy!" she squealed from excitement.

Nathaniel's face was drawn from a frantic evening without sleep. He slid from his saddle and picked up his child. He listened while Rebecca chattered about her new dress though her words fell on his deaf ears. His eyes were fixed on Abigail and the rod she held. Nathaniel shuffled across the porch to greet his wife. He held her with his open arm and gently kissed her cheek.

"When did this arrive?"

"Early this morning." Abigail hesitated, and then blurted her thoughts, "Must you ride again, Nathaniel?"

He began to answer, but Abigail continued, "You are exhausted. You have not eaten, and this is the third time in five days." She pounded her boot on the floor, "And this pace cannot continue or I will be...."

"Or you will be what?" His tone was stout. His face softened. "My dear Abigail, freedom comes when it is called. We know not of the time required. And what if I did not heed its call? Could you live with a condemnation of another of God's creatures simply because his skin color is different than ours?"

Abigail's eyes dropped to the floor. "But…."

Nathaniel held up his hand and lifted her chin. With a shake of his head he spoke, "No. We must do the work that is required of us – without food, hesitation, or sleep — or we are no different than those who bind them in slavery."

Rebecca's eyes widened at the mention of this word. Her meek voice mimicked her father, "Slavery…is an undone evil." Her parents' words were silenced by her spoken thought, but she paid them no mind. She skipped off the porch and repeated her phrase again. After the third time the pounding of approaching hooves silenced her.

Nathaniel grabbed the rod from Abigail's hand and rushed into the barn. He tossed it onto the top of a pile of straw and placed more to cover it. He was calming his agitated horse when the barn door flung open.

Abigail escorted two gentlemen into the building. The three men stood toe to toe without a word exchanged between them. Finally one of the visitors spoke.

"A long night for a ride was it not, Nathaniel?"

"What is the meaning of your visit?"

"We came for a drink of water. We have been on the hunt of two fugitive slaves and lost their trail just beyond your property." He pulled his face close to Nathaniel. His eyes narrowed. "Have you seen any colored men passing this way?"

"I have not." Nathaniel looked at Abigail, "Draw these men a cool drink and a bit of bread for their stomachs."

She took her cue to exit before the confrontation began. When she walked out of the barn, she searched for Rebecca. She rushed through the house, calling her name, but it was silent. She called her name again from the front porch. It was then she heard her voice. She saw her daughter talking quietly to a man who knelt before her. Abigail was relieved to find her daughter safe but wanted to remove her from the situation at hand.

"There you are," Abigail tried to sound calm. "Run along now into the house before you get your new dress dirty." She patted her on the bottom and gently nudged her toward the house.

The man tipped his hat to Abigail, "Ma'am." He walked to the barn and joined the others. Once inside the building, he yelled to the two men standing with Nathaniel, "We are wasting our time here. Let's ride."

The two men stopped in mid-sentence and rushed to follow their leader. Dust flew into the air from their horses' hooves as they rode in the opposite direction from which they came.

Nathaniel's eyes warned Abigail against words before his feet touched the porch floor. He knelt to his daughter. His tone was soft.

"Tell me your story."

"No story, only secrets." Rebecca giggled.

"Secrets are only among friends, Rebecca, and that man was not your friend." He hesitated, "Your mother saw you speaking together."

Rebecca's smile slid from her face. "But Daddy, he just asked me if I had seen any colored men."

"And what was your answer?"

"I asked him what color he was talking about." Once again, she giggled.

"What was his reply?"

"Oh, he said black or brown." She danced around the room, watching the calico print swirl as she moved. "You know what I said?"

A lump formed in Nathaniel's throat, as he shook his head *no*.

"I told him I have never seen the face of a black or brown man." She stopped twirling and smiled at her father.

"Rebecca, that was a kind thing to say, but why did you lie?"

"But, Daddy, I have never seen a black man's face before."

Nathaniel shook his head in disbelief. He tried to count the number of men that he had helped to freedom. He tried to recall how many had eaten dinner at his table but could not settle on an exact number.

"Rebecca, good Quaker girls do not speak lies."

"It's not a lie!" She answered defiantly.

"Rebecca...." Abigail tried to comfort her daughter.

"No, Mommy, it is not a lie! Daddy always makes them hide their faces. So I won't recognize them. I have never seen a black face."

Nathaniel rolled back on his heels and began to laugh. He picked Rebecca up and tossed her into the air.

"My wise little girl!" He laughed again. He looked at his wife, "She performs as her mother!"

After a hearty meal and a bath, Rebecca fell asleep in her father's arms. He carried her to her bed and slipped a coverlet over her body. Abigail was rocking beside the fireplace when he returned.

"She's too observant. It will only be a matter of time before she wants to be involved."

Nathaniel shook his head. "This is grave business and not that of a little girl."

"I agree, but her head is just as strong as her heart. She will want to do her part."

"I'll not discuss this further. You know more than you should."

"Nathaniel, I'm not suggesting she ride with you. Do not raise your voice. I am suggesting a small part, very small. You best be thinking of a way, for the day will come when she will ask and you must not hesitate in your reply."

A thin smile crossed Nathaniel's lips. "I will think on it. My heart knows you speak the truth, but it also hopes that day never comes."

George knelt by the glowing embers of his late autumn fire. He picked up a stick and wrote in the soft sand. Drops of water flooded his eyes as he stared at the word scribbled on the ground. The letters G-O-R-G-Ǝ stared back at him. He smiled at his old spelling with the backward facing E. It was his trademark, his way of saying goodbye. He knew this would be the final time he wrote those letters in Georgia soil. He gathered his sack and lifted his eyes.

"Freedom lies there," his thick finger pointed north. "George is a free man."

He walked the same path he traveled the last time he ran for freedom, but he did not stop to remove his neckband. A nervous sense of uneasiness slid down his back as he walked past the spot where he had been captured. He held his breath until his lungs burned.

After many cold, fire-less nights and days of walking, George saw his destination. He had memorized the instructions laid down by Lacey and knew he was growing close to the first safe house.

It was a large stone structure. In the second window of the top floor a lone candle flickered. Its glow could be seen from a far distance. George shook his head in disbelief that he had arrived safely, without opposition. His six-day walk through fields and swamp was worth it. He approached the dark side door as directed. His planned series of knocks were answered by the snap of the inside latch.

Without any light from the inside, George whispered into the darkness, "I, George, am free from slavery."

A soft male voice answered, "Welcome, George, to our freedom house."

George slipped through the door. He was given a hot cup of coffee, a blanket, and a soft pillow. In silence he was shown upstairs to a room without windows. A chest of drawers held a wash basin and pitcher, and a thunder jug was placed in the opposite corner. A loose floorboard was removed to reveal his place of rest for the next few days.

George slid into the narrow space and settled onto a soft down tick. He was asleep before the floorboard was replaced. His dreams were long and uninterrupted.

He woke to a lantern illuminating his face. "Mister...."

"Yes, sir," answered George.

"You have slept nearly a day away. Are you sick?"

"No, sir, young man."

"Come join us for a hot meal. Mother has a place set for you."

George climbed out of his security and followed the boy down a flight of stairs, around a corner, and into a dimly lit kitchen. The boy slid into his chair, which left only one seat intended for George. It was to the right of the man who answered the door, Simon Tuttle. George stopped before assuming the empty chair was intended for him.

54

After all, he had never been seated at such a lofty position at a proper table.

The gentleman of the house knew his thoughts and rose to invite George to be seated. "Please, sir," he spoke quietly, "be seated so that we may pray for your freedom and safety." He held out his hand as a silent gesture.

George slid into the empty chair. He folded his hands in prayer before him and glanced at all seated at the table.

Simon began to speak, "Dear Lord, we pray for your servant George before us. We pray you place a hedge of protection around him. Shower him with your grace and abundance as he begins this treacherous road to freedom. May you spur others to come behind him, and may you grant them wisdom. We thank you for the gifts of life, food, and health that you have given our family, and we pray, Lord, for strength to help us continue in your work. Bless the sweet hands that prepared this meal, and help it to give us courage and fortitude to do what must be done. In Your name, with Your blessing, Amen."

"Amen," George whispered in response to those around him. He looked at Simon and said, "And may God bless you for your sacrifices for me."

The meal was filled with light conversation. No mention of where George had come or his intended destination was discussed in front of the eight children. When the last of the boys was excused from the table, the two men were left to speak in confidence.

George told Simon his tale of Oak Bend, Lacey, Lilly, and his unsuccessful attempts for freedom. Simon listened without interruption. He was amazed at this slave's skill level of the English language.

George explained the significance of the three names that were circled in The Bugle. He spoke for much of the evening of his adoration for Lacey. He made no mention of the money or of his suspicions of Lilly's help. Lacey though young was intelligent, but the plan for freedom was too elaborate, too well planned, to be a child's scheme. George knew Lilly was the architect.

Simon listened until George grew silent. He was fascinated by his stories and could not imagine the life and hardships each slave endured. His passion to assist grew stronger with each slave's arrival.

"George, you will remain with us for three more days. Preparations need to be made and ensured for your safety to the next freedom house. You must stay in hiding. This home is under the watchful eyes of the Copperheads. All movement is monitored. We will do our best to hold your comfort, but naught can be done to speed the progress. Do you understand?"

George, for the first time in his life, answered a question without lowering his eyes or his stance, "Yes, sir, I understand."

Simon was aware of his intrepid response. He had witnessed many freed slaves evolve to the same conclusion. He patted the back of George's hand without a reply. He rose from the table and George followed.

Sleep did not come easy for George that night. His thoughts were restless and his mind wandered into an area in which it should not.

His body was in the middle of a field of lilies. Their fragrance was pungent and sweet. George stood still, listening to the sounds of nature that surrounded him. Suddenly, he found himself standing in a barn, covered with chains. He was encircled by angry voices, though their faces remained hidden. Soon the building was on fire and he struggled to free himself of the chains. The fire crept closer. The heat melted his flesh. The sound of his screaming voice tore him from the impending doom.

When he sat up, his head hit the floorboard. He settled back into his soft pillow and feather tick. He shivered from the dampness of sweat that surrounded him. He bent his thoughts on the innocence of Lacey's face and tried to slow his panicked breathing.

The luxury of sleep was stolen. He lay awake listening to the sounds of the house. Pops, creaks, and an occasional crack only goaded his desire to drift into slumber. He was stiff and irritable. Hours seemed to pass before he felt safe to lift the floorboard.

George crawled out of his cramped quarters. It took several tries before he could stand erect. His hand rubbed the knot on his forehead. He stood alone in the dark room, not knowing the time of day or night. He sighed and propped his fatigued body in a corner.

Soon he heard shuffling in the kitchen below him. He watched a dim light appear under the crack in the door. It became brighter until the door flew open wide. Simon was startled to see George sitting in the corner.

"Nightmares steal your pleasantness?"

"Yes, sir."

"It is common. They will lessen in time."

George smiled at his kindness. Mary appeared with a steaming bowl of clear water. In its bath was a knife.

"George," she whispered, "we must remove your marker. It will not be pleasant, for your skin has attached itself in several places." She knelt beside him as Simon fueled the lamp flame. "It appears this has been done before."

Her knowing smile made George laugh. "Yes, Ma'am. A few times."

She worked the sharp sterile knife until the last of his skin was freed from the chain. A bloody rag colored the water. The tag and chain turned the bowl scarlet, yet to George, the rattle sounded freedom.

Mary finished cleaning George's neck and covered his raw skin with an herb poultice. The bitter aroma caused his eyes to tear. She covered his wounds with Lady's Mantle and wrapped his neck loosely with strips of oiled cloth. The final covering was a piece of homespun muslin. The stiff fabric held the dressing in place.

She gave him a cup of hot tea. "Now drink this and let the herbs go to work. Lie down and rest until I have prepared you something to eat."

"I'm not hungry, Ma'am."

"I know, George, but you must keep your strength. You cannot allow your wounds to become infected. Your body must be strong to fight." Mary gathered her bowls, rags, and knife. "I'll bring you some soup. That will help you sleep."

After he lapped the bowl of chicken soup, filled with potatoes, carrots, turnips and rutabagas, he settled onto his feather tick. His neck burned from the trauma, yet he knew the pain would allow rest. Alone in his dark, quiet room, with his stomach and heart filled, George drifted into an easy sleep.

The next few days passed quickly and without any problems. Mary changed his dressing twice daily and the wounds were healing nicely. Each application required fewer bandages.

"By tomorrow," Mary said as she peeked under the cloth, "your neck should require minimum attention. It will be easy for you to do. But, George, you must keep it clean and dry. I will send enough bandages until you reach your next freedom house."

She glanced at her husband, "How long will it take?"

"About a week."

Nathaniel had set off the evening two days prior. His delayed homecoming made Abigail restless. Her eyes were set in the distance praying for his safe return.

The unsettled wind stirred the dry dirt around the foundation of their home.

Several men had arrived at dawn to finish a new barn. None spoke of Nathaniel's absence. The lack of questions fueled the growing feeling of Abigail's dread.

By lunch she had set a place for the men at a table under the shade of a large oak tree. Her eyes scanned the faces of these men — only three of the ten were known to her. Their gaze was set on the food before them. Without a word of thanks the meal was devoured.

Abigail watched from the safety of her back door. Two men were engaged in hushed discussion. The rest of the group clung to each spoken word. Occasionally one glanced toward Abigail. She slid through the back door and called Rebecca's name.

Panic rose to an uncomfortable level as she raced through the house calling for her only child. The lack of reply manifested in tears. She collapsed by an east window.

She caught a glimpse of a lone rider. She stood in hopes it was Nathaniel. She tripped down the back staircase and rushed out of the front door. The known rider opened his coat to reveal her hidden daughter. Abigail gasped. He grabbed her arm and pulled her onto the back of the horse.

The trio slid behind a row of pine trees and followed their course for cover. They entered a thicket that obscured the wood edge. Slowly and silently they moved on an unmarked path until the house was long from view.

The horse slowed to a stop. Abigail pulled her cloak from her face. Rebecca wiggled with excitement. The rider slid from his horse and helped the women to the soft dirt in a clearing. A ring of trees, wide from years of growth, surrounded the clearing.

The rider spoke softly to the open space, "Come. We are your servants."

Ten men disguised by the foliage stepped into view. Rebecca wiggled out of her mother's grip and ran to one of the men. Nathaniel lowered his body and embraced his daughter.

Abigail stood in silent awe. She knew not of this gathering place, of hurried rides, or of Rebecca's involvement. She watched as her daughter called the men to her. She pulled a note from her corset. Each man studied the contents and passed it to the one beside him. When all read the note, it was burned. The smoldering paper danced on a gentle breeze and settled at Abigail's feet. Rebecca gathered the charred tuft and scattered it in the growing wind.

The men slid through the dense underbrush. The sound of hooves filled the clearing. Within minutes, Nathaniel approached his wife.

"I apologize for the secrecy. It was brought to my attention that you were in danger."

Abigail opened her mouth to speak, but the sound of her daughter's voice halted her words. "Mother, the men at our house were not there to build. They came to destroy. Word came just before I reached the clearing."

Abigail scolded Rebecca with her tone. "You came to this place alone?"

Nathaniel knelt before his wife. He gently stroked her hand. "My dear, Abigail, this is grave business. We try not to involve all. Safety is in silence." He smiled and stood before Abigail. His grip did not change. "Forgive our daughter. She was only thinking of your protection."

"But, Nathaniel, she's only a child!"

"Do you remember our conversation just a few years ago? You knew then that Rebecca wanted to become involved."

He motioned for Rebecca to join their circle. "She is not in danger. Her part is at the beginning and not discovered. She receives word in secret from Daniel, who has remained in contact with a Southern gentleman. Word of the slave's journey comes through him. His name is Simon Tuttle. Along with his wife, Mary, they have aided many slaves to freedom. It is part of a small, yet mighty, network of people who are devoted to the cause. Until now, Rebecca and I have been able to keep you protected...until today."

Nathaniel's eyes lifted to the sky. His sigh was heavy as he began to explain. "Rebecca received word of three men traveling together. They have infiltrated our band, managing to deceive many along the way. We had taken them in, shown them the way. They traveled with us to the railroad just last evening. The night went as planned until the faces of the two black slaves appeared out of the train car. Shots were fired. Confusion ensued. When all was settled, both slaves had been killed and two of the imposters. One of the men escaped on foot. We tracked him

62

for nearly twelve hours until we caught up to him. With his dying breath, he spilled his plan for your life."

Abigail's face was paste-white. Tiny beads of sweat covered her skin. Her hands had a tight grip on Rebecca.

Nathaniel tried to calm her, "Abigail, all ends well. We sent a rider to come for you. Your wise reactions brought you to the front of the house. We were able to save you without notice." His smile was warm, yet anger built in Abigail.

"I knew this business was dangerous. I do not agree to involve our child. Your poor judgment has brought a flurry of suspicions on our family. Not to mention the danger you have thrown upon us. I am not in agreement with your decisions, yet what shall I do? My involvement is now reflexive, but our daughter? Oh, Nathaniel!" Abigail slid to the ground, buckling under her weakened knees.

Rebecca sat before her mother. "It was through my insistence that Father finally conceded. I have been pleading for a part for nearly three years. I gave him no choice." She took her mother's hand, "Although your part of ignorance was permitted, you know and believe in this cause. You also have done your part, Mother."

"I do not agree with the danger in which you so eagerly place yourself, Rebecca."

"Danger? What is danger when human rights are bought and sold? These men, women, and children are not given a choice. They live their lives as servants of others, naught for a wage, nor honor, but for duty – duty to a master who sees his way to beat and torture his property into submission. Our Lord does not agree with this behavior and I willingly do my part, no matter how small, to see this injustice undone." Tears streamed down her face.

Abigail was stuck by her daughter's resolve. She swelled with pride of her twelve-year-old daughter's maturity. Rebecca's words were spoken in love, yet with conviction. They touched Abigail and she smiled at her daughter.

"You have much of your father within you. You have his eloquent speech and fortitude. How can I argue?" She stood and straightened her dress. "Let's go home."

Without a horse the walk took several hours. They arrived at their property line at dusk. Orange blush filled the sky. Nathaniel ran to the top of a knoll. In the distance he saw all that remained of their home; a few beams standing in the midst of glowing embers.

The following morning George and Simon set off before sunrise. As promised an extra bag of herbs and clean dressing were nestled beside strips of dried meat, apples, and peanuts.

Mary filled George's water jug with fresh spring water and replaced his tattered blanket with one of soft wool. A few extra strips of clean dressing were placed inside his bedding roll.

George crawled inside the limited space between the false and true bottom of the buckboard. Simon tossed several bales of hay on top of the secret opening. Bits of chaff made their way through the open cracks of the floorboards, making the journey for George a long, irritating one.

The road was rough, jarring, and extremely slow. To help conceal his true intentions, Simon attached one of his cows to the back of the buckboard. It looked as though he was leading his heifer to the market, and since the most active sale barn was four days' ride, his cover seemed flawless.

By the time the men arrived at a safe place to stop for the night, George was immobile. His body would not obey his will to crawl out of his hiding place. Simon helped him to his feet.

"It is not an easy ride, George."

All he could manage was, "No, sir."

They spoke in hushed voices over a paltry fire. A pot of beans, dried beef, and a shared apple were dinner. No matter how meager, it had enough sustenance to allow for a good night's rest. Simon guarded the first half of the night while George dreamed of freedom. The bawl of a lone coyote woke George from a sound sleep. It was midnight.

"Did you hear that?" George questioned his caretaker.

Simon poked at the dying embers. "Just sounds of the night. Go back to sleep."

"I believe I am fully awake now, sir. Your turn now. Go rest a bit. I'll wake you in the mornin'."

Exhausted, Simon patted George on the back, "I will take that advice, Mr. George. Thank you and good night."

Soon the sound of Simon's snores filled the quiet woods. The coyote was not heard again.

Before the light of dawn, George nestled into the non-comfort of his narrow space in the wagon. Simon whistled and hummed as the second day's journey began.

By noon, Simon's shoulders were dappled with rain, and within an hour the sky let loose of its fury. Lightning and thunder made rough traveling with the cow. She fought their forward movement. Simon worried that she sensed danger.

They reached the banks of the South Edisto River at nearly four o'clock. The weighed barge was docked on the opposite shore. A wagon with a young mother and child struggled to cross the mud onto dry land. The crack of the whips caused their horses to rear in defiance. With the final lash, the wooden spokes were freed from the soft earth. It took only a few minutes to settle the horses and for the pair to be on their way. The captain turned his attention to the opposing shore and his next fare.

The strong tide mingled with the day's rain as it hurried to meet the salt water of St. Helena Sound. The boat rocked while the men struggled to bring the cargo aboard. The smell of brackish water brought George a sense of peace. His rain-soaked body, pricked with hay, drifted to sleep from the boat's rocking motion on the outgoing tide.

Simon's calloused fingers held George's chain and slave tag. His lowered eyes followed each move of the barge captain. At a moment of inattention, Simon tossed the tag and chain into the dark water. He lifted his eyes toward Otter Island and whispered a silent prayer for those held there.

The captain shouted the order, "Steady your girl. The shore's a comin'."

The narrow barge slammed into the dock on the opposite riverbank. George was startled from his slumber. The horse pulled the wagon through the mud to dry earth. Simon waved to the captain though he did not turn around. His thoughts were bent on the safety of the woods, not the exposure of the open water.

George struggled to move his hips but was held fast by the floorboards. His feet tingled. He closed his eyes and thought of Lacey.

13

GEORGE

Tobias sat on the shoreline of Otter Island. Beside him were three faint lines drawn in the sand signifying the number of days he spent motionless on the west bank. Sketched somewhere on the eastern shore were four more hash marks. The morning's rain soothed his sunbaked skin and moistened his blistered lips. It was the first drink he had in seven days.

Weary from hunger he forced his body to his knees. His bloody toes dug into the coarse sand. Shell shards and bits of pumiced stone embedded in his feet. He rocked back and forth until finally he managed to stand. His vision narrowed and faded to grey. He lifted his arms to steady his balance, wobbling and stumbling, until his body settled into an upright position.

He lifted his eyes to the east and caught sight of a British ship as it sailed from the shore. Random splashes could still be seen from the bow and stern. Men ran wildly along the rail to throw off their assailants. He closed his eyes from the vision; that had been him only eight days prior.

It was nearly four weeks ago that he met a young sea captain at a port in Philadelphia. With sugared promises of return to his mother country ringing in his ears, Tobias willingly walked onto the deck of *The Clara*.

Ignorant with trust, he boasted to all others on board, "In a few months, brotha, we will be home...and free." He was met with gruff grunts and turned faces. "Why empty eyes, brothas? Wees a goin' home."

The Clara stopped at numerous ports as it made its way down the eastern shoreline of America. The ship was filled with anxious slaves that joined Tobias and the wary others on board who feared to return to their plantation owners since abandoning them for the war. Many volunteered to help the vessel maneuver through the uncharted waters with great success. The young captain appeared grateful for their shared knowledge and repaid them with food scraps, though many were immediately overcome with dysentery.

After sailing for three days the ship turned inland once again. Tobias approached the captain, "Another port, suh?"

"A resting spot, Tobias."

"Rest from what, suh? We needs to get home."

The captain chuckled at his innocence. "How old are you, Tobias?"

"Suh?"

"When were you born?"

"In the spring rains twenty-seven years ago."

"And how long were you a slave?"

Tobias narrowed his eyes as he counted, "Twelve springs, suh." He hesitated, and then added, "Yes, suh. I'sa been a slave for twelve springs."

69

"And why do you want to return to Africa? What is there for you?"

Tobias' eyes flooded with tears. The drops moistened his bare chest as he spoke, "My momma, suh. My momma's there."

"What about your father?"

"No, suh. He was taken same day as me. I ain't never seen him since."

The captain never responded.

Tobias watched as the ship moved closer to the water's edge. Silhouettes of people jumping and dancing moved through the shoreline shadows. Tobias smiled at the glorious greeting.

As the vessel moved closer, the decimation of Otter Island was evident. Dead bodies littered the water's edge. Bull sharks pulled at their extremities to feed their young. The waves held a sickening shade of red.

Tobias ran toward the captain but was halted by guns. "Suh! Suh, what is this?"

The cocked guns were forced to his chest. Not a word was spoken and Tobias finally understood.

The sound of the sand grinding the ship to a halt echoed death to all who stood on the bow. One by one the slaves were forced from the vessel. They jumped from the plank to a shelf only ten feet deep. Swarms of bull sharks lingered for an easy meal. Screams of the bitten flooded the air.

Tobias swam through four pools of blood. His body was driven to the safety of the shore, yet his eyes were filled with those swimming in the opposite direction. In five feet of water his leg brushed against the rough skin of a shark. In a moment, the man beside him disappeared as the rush of water into his lungs snuffed his screams.

The erratic motion of frenzied swimming continued long after Tobias' stomach hit the sand. Nearly hysterical, he pulled his body out of the water. When he turned to face *The Clara,* his mind denied what his eyes saw. The ship had begun to sail away from the island. The sides of the hull were covered with men clinging to the ship for deliverance. One by one, the captain's deckhands hoisted their bodies to rail. Just as their hands neared the top, a long blade severed their fingers. Their shocked bodies tumbled into the water amid the shark's feeding frenzy. By morning, blood stained the eastern sands of Otter Island. The trash line was littered with kelp, twigs, and oyster shells amid fingers and flesh of the dead.

Exhausted, Tobias collapsed on the ground. The wind whispered voices of rancorous ghosts as it rushed through the reeds and pursued the sea. He watched the island veterans bury the remains of the lost and forgotten, all together without names.

An old man, missing both arms, stumbled to his side. "Only a few have made it."

Tobias was too spent to do anything but grunt.

"Yep," he continued, "only a few made it back to the mother country."

Now he had Tobias' attention. "What say you old man?"

"The ship comes once a week. Yep, suh, once a week. Drops some off, picks some up. If yous gets picked up, yous a goin' back. Goin' back home to…." his cough stole his words.

"You say the ship comes back once a week?"

The old man shook his head, stood, stumbled to the water's edge, and dove in headfirst. He never screamed when he was pulled under. A pool of reddened water marked his eternal spot. Tobias watched in silent horror as the sharks continued to circle. Yesterday was a good feeding day; today was a bit slimmer.

Six days later the ship reappeared. Tobias was determined to reach the vessel and speak to the captain. Fear of the sharks was less than the fear of dying from scurvy or starvation on this forgotten ground. He was certain he could persuade the young captain to return the contraband to Africa unscathed.

He listened as the ship's hull scraped the edge of the shelf. The sound of a horn blast moved the staff into a well-rehearsed motion. Within moments the water was crammed with splashes, screams, and fins.

Tobias jumped vigorously into the oncoming waves. His strokes were deliberate as he made his way through the crowded water. The wood of the ship was covered in sea slime, making it difficult to climb. The sharpness of the barnacles tore at his skin as he hoisted his body up remnants of a dangling rope. His drained energy was forced to submission until he flung his weathered body onto the deck of *The Clara.*

His eyes met the barrel of a gun as he forced his body to stand. "I needs to see the captain!" he shouted with the last burst of energy.

Two men dragged his body to the captain. When Tobias lifted his eyes, surprise silenced his words. Before him stood an elderly man, not the young captain he expected.

The old salt spoke in a gruff voice, "You wanted to speak to me?"

Tobias' thoughts were jumbled. His words were spoken in a drunken manner, forced through exhaustion, without food and water. The captain quickly lost patience and dismissed him. Before Tobias could pull together his expressions and force them from his lips, he was tossed into the water.

He swam to shore in slow motion. Twice he hit the nose of an assailing bull shark, only to have them retreat. It wasn't until he lurched onto the sand that he realized his fingers were gone. With the beach speckled red with his own blood, he couldn't recall the blade. He lifted his damaged limbs to inspect his loss; only his thumbs remained.

Whispers of a passerby rang in his ear, "Your fate has been set. No more can you pursue. The way home is gone. Slipped through your fingers." He folded to the sand and wept.

Tobias shook the sordid memory from his mind. He stumbled along the western shore. The Edisto River was fierce in its determination to catch the ebbing tide as bull sharks crowded its rapid current. He had watched several men dive to their end over the past few days, overcome by either the monster or the rip tide. Either one was a certain death.

He staggered along the raging waves. They pulled the rough sand from beneath his feet, making it difficult to stay erect. He felt coolness on his left foot. Resting on the top was a slave tag attached to a chain. He lifted it with his thumbs and fumbled to read the inscription.

"George," he whispered. He flipped the tag over and read the front, "Oak Bend."

It had been four days since Simon carefully smuggled George over the South Edisto River. The tag had been forced to the sands of Otter Island by the outgoing tide, and as fate would have it, Tobias, a learned man, found it.

Tobias lifted the tag into the air and laughed. His words were shouted in his native tongue, "Brother. May your flight for freedom be without problem, your life be long, and your love be deep. May God keep you!" He danced until his feet could hold him no longer.

I t took three years to complete the Kristols' new home. Nathaniel used the unfortunate loss to fuel the fire in his soul. He built many of the basic necessities quickly, but Nathaniel took pride in the tedious. The design of hidden rooms, secret passageways, and the lookout tower was centered on his family's voluntary business — slave smuggling.

Since the fire, Rebecca became a crucial abolitionist. Abigail joined her, at first for assured safety, but as time progressed the need of their paired involvement was essential. Through the past several years the number of slaves that had moved through their home had grown to hundreds. With each freed slave the Copperheads' plan was thwarted, and the number of enemies against the Kristols grew.

Most freedom flights went as clockwork. A few close calls kept the men alert. All were cautious of their tongues and none spoke to strangers. The Anti-Slavery Movement in Salem, Ohio, was alive and well.

Since the completion of their new home, the Kristol family moved farther into seclusion. Hired help was closely supervised and worked under a blanket of suspicion. Nathaniel finished the majority of the carpentry alone.

By spring the strict watch became somewhat relaxed. Although strangers were not greeted without vigilant glances, they were welcomed. Rebecca had grown into a beautiful young woman of fifteen, though she had no interest in suitors. She discarded her romantic desires- for her true love was freedom for the unjust.

The routine of slave smuggling had become second nature to the family. Rebecca would ride into town for news from her sources, mostly alone, though at times escorted by her mother to divert suspicion. The family's participation was suspected but not proven, which made the Copperheads anxious and desperate. All went as planned until one mission.

It was mid-afternoon in late May. A harried rider approached the Kristols' home. His horse foamed from riding hard. Nathaniel greeted the man with a cool drink for both him and the steed.

The man spoke from his saddle, "They are coming on the early train." His speech was hushed and hurried. "There was no time for warning. I have ridden from Sebring to plead your assistance."

Nathaniel rushed to the barn and jumped on his unsaddled horse. He rode quickly past the west window.

"Abigail! Abigail!" His horse spun in tight circles.

Abigail opened the upstairs window. She smiled at her handsome husband.

He tossed his words to her quickly, "We must ride. My aid is requested. Look for my return after sunset." The riders disappeared into the row of pine trees.

Abigail was alone in the house. Rebecca had left for Salem a few hours before. They had received word that three men were heading north, and they needed to make contact with Daniel Hise for the details. Her soon return was expected.

Abigail fanned the freshly washed sheets over the straw mattress. She drew in a deep breath of the spring air carried through the fabric. She straightened the wrinkles, gathered the winter coverlet, and replaced it with a summer spread.

She laughed, "It may be a bit soon to use the summer bedding, but after this winter I'm in need of a lighter load." She wondered if she was talking about the bedding or life – either was correct.

She carried the heavy coverlet to the clothesline. The edges of the wool skirted the ground from its weight. She supported the cord with a prop fashioned from a stout maple limb. She swung her rug beater at the dusty fabric. Before she finished thrashing the coverlet, eight men on horses surrounded her. Her terrified eyes screamed, but her throat was silent.

"What do you want?" Her voice quivered as she spoke.

"Where is Nathaniel?"

"What concern is that of yours?" Her hands wrapped tighter around her weapon.

"Where is Nathaniel?" the man repeated.

"I see no reason to speak with you. I owe you no explanation."

The leather of his saddle groaned under his movement. He leaned forward and spoke through clenched teeth, "I demand to know his whereabouts."

"He went to town," she answered in disgust, "for some supplies for the cattle." She added, "Not that it is any business of yours." She made a few steps forward and was stopped by one of the men. He pulled the rug beater from her hand before she had a chance to strike.

They shouted questions about Nathaniel. She refused to answer. Their tone became more agitated at each refusal. They slid from their horses one by one, each moving dangerously close to her. She tried to run but was overcome by one of the men. He forced her to the ground.

He sneered as he spoke inches from her face, "And where is your innocent Rebecca?"

The mockery in his voice provoked her to action. She lunged at his face. Her fingernails raked across his eyes. Blood clouded his vision immediately.

"What have you done to my daughter?" she shouted through her tears.

No answer came from the crowd. They gathered around her and began to strike her. She fought valiantly, but her strength was no match for the number of enraged men. The final blow came from her clothesline prop.

Their questions continued as her blood colored the dirt. She tried to pull herself away from her assailants to no avail. She collapsed on the ground with her face smothered in the gore.

The men rode around her limp body in a tight circle of triumph. The horses pounded the dirt with their hooves. The leader broke off from the pack and led the men to the south. The last man tossed a cluster of rolled parchment paper. It was tied with a piece of twine. The bundle rolled and rested against Abigail's body, resting in her growing blood.

Rebecca rode from Salem in an easy gallop. She had received the information about the slaves, and they were not due to arrive for two days. She was relieved to have a bit of a rest for her family.

The past few weeks had been filled with action. Not only had they successfully helped ten men on the way to freedom, but also the family received word through Daniel that three brothers had crossed the border to Canada. They survived their quest from slavery to freedom. The news lit Rebecca's heart. She could not wait to share it with her mother.

The minute the thought of Abigail came to her she was filled with anxiety. She forced her horse to press hard. The eventual sight of her home gave a pinch of relief. Her horse seemed to tense as they rode closer.

Rebecca slid off the saddle and ran into the house. The returned silence of her calling made her uneasy. She ran up the back flight of the stairs, past the wall of hidden rooms concealed behind raised panels. She ran from room to room calling to Abigail. The silence was deafening.

She ran to an open window in her bedroom and looked outside. Her eyes fell on her mother lying in a pool of blood. Her feet carried her down the stairs and out of the door without a thought. Stricken by panic, she was unable to breathe. She slid to the ground beside her mother and whispered her name. No reply came.

Rebecca held her mother's body close to her and cried until darkness covered them. Her ears were deaf to the sound of her father's galloping horse.

eorge woke to the sound of well-planned knocks inches from his face. He slid the lock open. Simon's smile was wide.

"We are on the private property of a dear friend. Please come sit a spell on the bench and keep me company."

George groaned as he slid his stiff body from hidden safety. "I could use with a bit of fresh air." He climbed beside Simon, "Thank you, sir."

They traveled through the four-thousand-acre plantation. Thick vegetation hindered fast travel, but the change was welcomed. The pair sat in silence as the wagon jarred along a sparsely used path. Palmetto palms slapped their faces. Resurrection ferns responded to the recent rain and covered the live oak's dangling limbs with their foliage. Warm puffs of air were encased in the coming cooler winds. Autumn was sliding to a memory.

"Sir?" George finally whispered. "Are we gettin' close?"

Simon smiled at his disguised anxiousness. "We will rest tonight in the safety of this land. Tomorrow we must travel through three towns full of prying eyes and listening ears. It will be the most taxing day." Simon sighed and patted the back of his leathered skin. "You will have to remain hidden all day and into the late evening. I am sorry, for your day will be rough.

George's shoulders sank from the weight of worry. He forced his words to sound optimistic, "It is a small price to pay for freedom, Mr. Simon. Yep, a small price."

"Freedom...it is a grand word, George."

"Yes, sir. 'Tis a grand word. Soon George is a free man." A smile lit his face. His posture straightened as he hummed a Gospel tune.

Simon tapped his foot and joined the familiar words. Within a few bars, the men sang in harmony. Their songs continued until it was time to settle their campsite for the evening. They watched the sun set with the last sip of coffee.

Knowing of tomorrow's peril, both men slept sound. The night's whispers fell on deaf ears. Neither stirred until dawn's first light.

With the wagon packed quickly, George slid silently into the false bottom of the buckboard. The snap of the lock gave a sense of security. With a whistle to the horse, the wagon began to creep forward.

George lay awake listening to each sound from the outside world. His toes caressed the box that Lilly gave him. He whispered a silent prayer for her well-being and for his safe passage.

An accusatory shout from alongside the wagon made Simon halt their movement. Within a few moments several men shouted questions to Simon.

"What news of you?" one man asked.

Simon followed the well-rehearsed script. "I'm taking this heifer to the market in Doilsburg."

"You are a long way off your path." Another voice hissed.

"No sir, this is my chosen way." Simon continued, "The road is less traveled and much flatter for her tired feet."

The men grumbled among themselves. Simon took this opportunity to snap the horse into movement.

"Good day, gentlemen," he tossed over his shoulder without looking. No reply from the group came.

George swallowed hard from the uneventful ordeal. He hoped it would be the final meeting of these men, but he felt the weight grow in his heart. Simon and George had not heard the last from these watchful eyes.

After a quiet hour Simon began to sing. George's throat closed from nerves. He fought hard to suppress a cough. Simon's melodic warning continued:

Watching, waiting, six men are they
Tempting and prodding for you today.
Be wary and silent as you pray
The hunters are gatherers and come to slay.

No cause will be given for them to see
A weary lone traveler with none but he.
Safety of passage will come my way
Silence is golden, oh Lord I pray.

Simon stopped singing and greeted a nearby witness, "Good morning, Ma'am. 'Tis a fine day for the market."

The woman's reply was muffled and far from their wagon. George sighed with relief. After a few minutes, Simon began his tune.

The six are now seven and gathering strength.
They're staying their distance but holding their weight.
Guns and now fire, I must be aware
For silence is golden, the Lord doth declare.

His words stopped but he continued to hum the tune. He abandoned the warning words and sang the true Gospel words. Hearing Simon sing the familiar song calmed George's nerves until suddenly the song and wagon stopped.

"What is the meaning of this juncture?" His tone was loud and irritable. "I will not make the market to sell my ware if I must be halted for your questions."

He whistled to the horse but stopped when a shot rang out. The horse reared and refused to settle. Simon struggled to gain control. Through the slats of the sideboard, George saw the growing flame. The men circled the wagon.

"Why travel so far to sell your heifer? Have you not passed several markets in your travels?"

"Yes, but the Doilsburg sale draws the largest crowd. I have sold several calves, steers, and heifers there. It is worth the trip for a larger profit."

"Why such a large buckboard to bring only one heifer? Surely a smaller wagon would have held your supplies."

"This is the only wagon I own gentleman. I am a man of little means and every token, as well as minute, is precious to me." He waved off his hand. "Now before you come closer and catch my hay on fire, I bid for your acceptance to allow passage."

The men began to grumble. Three men slid from their horses and slowly circled the wagon. Finally satisfied that no one could be hiding in the three bales of hay, they waved Simon through.

One of the men mocked, "We will bid on your fine heifer in Doilsburg." The crowd erupted into laughter.

Once again, George exhaled. His body tingled from hindered movement. *A small price to pay*, he thought. He forced his eyes to close as Simon resumed his Gospel song.

16

*N*athaniel and Rebecca brought Abigail's body to Hope Cemetery in Salem. No one followed. Only the minister accompanied the diminished Kristol family.

Nathaniel asked the gravedigger for permission to help with the burrowing. The drunken man gladly accepted the offering.

A short distance away, Rebecca watched in silence while the men opened the earth to receive her mother's body. The casket wrapped in long ropes was slowly lowered into the ground. The few steps to reach the edge of Abigail's resting place seemed to take an hour of her day. Her hand trembled as she tossed a bouquet of pink roses onto the polished box. She hid her face from the void as the first shovel of the soft earth landed on the coffer. She suppressed her tears by exploring the other memorials.

The cemetery was established in 1803. Several obelisks stood as a testament from the ones who loved and remembered the buried. Trees and shrubs were planted by their memorials and flowers speckled the landscape.

A few earthen mounds were void of grass. Even the crabgrass refused to cover them. The graves were small; those of children, she thought. Rebecca stroked their headstones and whispered a prayer for the grieving family.

One memorial, recently placed, made her pause. It was carved of white marble and stood over four feet tall. A large winged bird placed at the top peak sat above the oversized word — UNION. The curved powder horn, sword, and officer tassels were crisp and skillfully done. It was the headstone of J.W. McConnell, a colonel of the 115th regiment.

Rebecca was stiff in thought. She was unaware of her consistent hum until her father placed his arm around her shoulder.

"Shall we go home, Rebecca?"

"Yes, Father. I am ready."

They walked past her mother's heaped gravesite. Rebecca placed the final pink rose on the brown dirt. She pressed her hand into its softness, leaving an impression.

"Goodbye, Mother. I will visit you often."

Nathaniel mimicked his daughter's imprint. Tears covered his cheeks. He whispered, "Always, my love. Always."

They traveled south to their home by way of Unserheim.

Daniel and his wife greeted the pair with open arms. Margaret led Rebecca into the kitchen while the men spoke quietly in the library. Talk of revenge and responsibility was thwarted by Daniel's quiet confidence of God's judgment.

"We must be faithful, Nathaniel. Abigail's death cannot be in vain. It is up to our Lord for judgment, not us."

"My mind hears your words, Daniel, but my heart does not. I feel I cannot continue without her. She was the paste that held us together."

"Then Rebecca must become that substance."

"No!" Nathaniel shouted. "I will not allow it."

The men were startled by the sound of Rebecca's innocent voice, "And what of me? Do I not have a voice?" She knelt to the floor in front of her father. "Father, I also am angry and black with mourning. Yet we all knew the danger. Mother willingly accepted it. She held our secrets to her death. We cannot turn back on her honor. I am deeply saddened, but in her death, I gather her strength. She will help guide us and keep us safe. These men cannot win by using death as a tool. They do not travel with the Lord's blessing. We may be against the law of the land and its rules on slavery, but I choose to answer to a higher power. God will give us courage…or I will die trying."

Nathaniel could not speak. Pride hindered his speech. Rebecca's strength and courage would not yield. He kissed her forehead and lifted her chin.

"You carry your mother's will and determination."

Daniel smiled, "And beauty." He looked at Rebecca, "You are wise beyond your years."

Hushed conversation filled the evening. Daniel spoke of hidden dangers in the glen. Rebecca and Nathaniel were filled with awe by his words. This news was unknown to them.

"We have an infiltrator or maybe several in our midst. They come to the clearing using our unmarked paths. They carry iron rods, bearing my mark, and yet I tell you, not by my hand were they made. Their faces change. They come swearing allegiance by the ones prior. Hatred is not masked by innocence!" He hung his head in defeat.

"When did this begin, Daniel? Why have we not heard of this until now?

"We thought you were safe. Your role in the freedom fight was well defined. Rebecca or Abigail gathered the news of a coming slave. A rod appeared at the time of the next day's train. You had your group of riders that you then placed rods by their door. A meeting in the glen gave instructions to the number of the rail car…." His words became hushed as he leaned closer to their faces. "All went as planned until a strange face appeared in a clearing meeting."

Daniel leaned his head back into the comfort of the chair and told Rebecca and Nathaniel his tale.

"Eight days ago a meeting was held in the glen. Many new faces were seen in the gathering. Conversation was kept light, without specifics, for I was fearful of attentive eyes. As I spoke, I tried to memorize the new faces. A few rose to speak of their opinions of the laws of our land.

"One young man commanded my attention. He was poised and confident in his words. They rolled from his lips with unbridled passion. They rose and fell with pitch and dynamics, yet his arms remained crossed as he held an iron rod. Only once did he open his hand to set his point off into the wind. His rod fell to the ground, and off flew the tip.

"It was curious to me that he was unaware of how useless he had rendered his weapon. Certainly he could strike with it, and even kill a man, but with the point lying unnoticed in the grass, no slave could be freed. He left without a care.

"After the crowd dwindled to the few that were originally invited, I gathered the cold tip from the earth. What I saw, Nathaniel, left me breathless. For it was fashioned as one of mine, but was naught by my hand." Daniel explained far into the late hours why this discovery was so poignant.

When the slave smuggling in Salem became an organized choir of people, the iron rod was used to signify the bearer's intentional belief and devotion to the cause. Many men met in secret to discuss what could be done to help aid in the freedom of a man who desired it. Without a word the group would appear, each with a staff of iron.

To ensure the men were trustworthy, Daniel made each rod in his blacksmith shop. He ground the tip of the rod to a narrow, flattened edge similar to that of an ax. With the final strike on the glowing iron, his maker's mark was visible. Daniel would only speak to the men if all held his mark. Never had his rod been duplicated, and the symbol of membership remained unspoken, yet so clearly visible.

He chose the rod because it held multiple uses. Besides an outward show of belonging, it was fashioned to slide into the doors of the railroad cars. With one fluid motion, the rod slid between the doors and broke the lock. The slave listened for this unspoken announcement as his call to freedom. He would jump from his place of hiding, leap through the open door, and join the men for the next phase of his covert journey. As a last resort, the rod also made a good weapon.

The liberty trail began deep in the South. Several safe houses were established along an unmarked path. It was the slave's responsibility to make his way to the first house. Once safe inside, a predetermined path was chosen for the slave. The homeowner, as a member of the Anti-Slavery Movement, took his life into his own hands to aid the man to safety.

The flight was dangerous, not only for the slave but also for the man who chose to lead him to liberty. Many men lost their lives as they traveled, or returned home to find their homes burned and their families slaughtered — all in the name of independence. Yet the safe houses remained a shelter signifying respite by a single candle lit in the second window on the upper floor. As the freedom seeker came to the door, a blue-colored bonnet designated the safe entrance.

A series of knocks and taps alerted the homeowner to the slave's intentions. The landowner asked questions from behind a locked door. If they were answered properly, the slave was invited into the house. Everyday items — rods, bonnets, newspapers, statuary, coins, and candles were used as symbols and tools for support. The masterful labyrinth was brilliantly designed, and success would have been higher if it weren't for the Copperheads.

The Copperheads were a group of Southern sympathizers. They believed in the right of slavery. They followed the law of the land and fought valiantly to uphold it. They viewed their opposition as unpatriotic, archaic, and weak. They believed the slave owners paid good money for their "property" and were well within their rights to fight to keep it. They felt secure in their position until the rise of a tall man from Illinois. They despised Abraham Lincoln and all his views – especially on slavery.

The faction had many unsuccessful attempts to infiltrate the Underground Railroad. The Anti-Slavery group in Salem, comprised mostly of Quakers, was shrewd and suspicious. The Copperheads' effort to blend in was easily noticed and avoided, until Hanna Prenstrum became active.

Hanna moved to Ohio four years after she was married. Her husband was originally from the Ohio Valley and longed to return to the family land. Hanna reluctantly left her home in Georgia, and her sister, Camellia Ward. The values of a Southern plantation owner were deeply engrained into her subconscious. She viewed the slaves as ones without rights, property of those who paid for them. Her brother-in-law Samuel shared her opinions while her sister was less severe since the birth of her daughters.

Hanna was a plump, sour, and harsh woman. Masculine overtones laced with hatred and bitterness were at the core of her words. She enjoyed control over others and used it as often as possible. Her staff equally hated and respected her, and she always got what she wanted — *always*.

Assuming the responsibility as ringleader of the local Copperheads before it was extended to her demonstrated her assertive nature. In her mind it was the only way to be certain of success. She spent the next few weeks assembling her team.

Joseph Whishas was her first recruit. He had strong ties in the South and was a fervent patriot. He believed the Underground Railroad would dismantle the country, and he spoke against it at any opportunity. No one questioned his loyalty to the Copperheads after he took part in last year's tar and feathering of a Quaker man. He held belief in God but felt a deeper connection to the power of the state and government — as long as his own views shadowed theirs.

Once given the authority, he visited many comrades and recruited their help. With little need to convince, most of the men leapt into action. They had spent too many idle hours watching as their town became a channel for illegal slave smuggling, and they were outraged.

Within three weeks the small band of angered men met for the first time in Hanna's barn. Hanna set in motion a well-laid plan. She separated the men into four groups – Watchers, Moles, Spoilers, and Eradicators.

The Watchers were four business owners in town. Their job was to listen to all conversations and be alert for information-gatherers like Rebecca and Abigail. Once they collected pertinent information of an attempt to free a slave they sent for the Moles.

The Moles were the most respected of the group. This trio was made up of Trey Cabot, a young man of twenty; John Kinrye, a gentleman of thirty-one; and Jesal Hiram, an esteemed religious man of sixty. All were attending Quakers in name only. The strict beliefs of the church had long become detached from their own though they maintained their positions for the benefit of connection.

Once the Moles successfully infiltrated the freedom fighters, they passed their information onto the Spoilers.

This was the largest number of Hanna's henchmen. The sheer size and strength of this unit screamed intimidation. With their number of twelve increasing on each ride, they quickly gained the respect of the assembly.

The last corps was the smallest. Their number was only two. They were the ruthless sector, the Eradicators, chosen for their lack of conscience. Murder came easily to them. Often they rode with the Spoilers but appeared through the crowd for their one and only purpose.

For several months Hanna held her band of Copperheads at bay. She wanted to be certain her plans would run like a well-oiled machine without question. In early August, they were ready to strike.

After successful information gathering, the Spoilers and Eradicators were sent to the Nerale house. They found Dorothy alone with her children. When she refused to tell of the whereabouts of her husband Jacob, the Eradicators were permitted to perform.

Dorothy held fast after being badly beaten, but when she heard the screams of her baby, she blurted out his location. Satisfied with the information, the Spoilers rode to the tracks. Only two men remained with Dorothy.

Three of the Spoilers rode ahead of the rest. They joined the group with a show of their rods. Relieved they were friends, Nathaniel opened the rail car door. Two black slaves jumped out of the train, but before they climbed onto the back of a horse, the men struck.

Nathaniel crumpled to the ground. His body fell limp from the force of his opponent's rod. Shouts of victory and hatred filled the air. The number of Spoilers quickly overcame Nathaniel's small band. Two more men slid to the ground. Their blood littered the swinging door of the railcar.

The train jerked forward. The squeal of the release was deafening. Stunned by the ease with which the Copperheads overcame them, the injured men stood still as they watched the Spoilers drag the slaves into the darkness.

When Nathaniel woke, he was with Jacob. They approached the Nerales' dark house in silence. The horror of Dorothy's children clinging to their mother's dead body was unbearable for Jacob. He was filled with rage and disappeared into the night. The next morning his beaten body was found swinging from a tree.

Daniel's words interrupted Nathaniel's thoughts. "I fear that with each intercepted slave, Hanna gains more confidence. Her men are thoughtless vessels of murder. Her number of supporters has continued to grow." He shook his head, "We must be diligent. We must be wary. We must stand united and strong."

When Simon and George entered the city of Doilsburg, it was two hours before sunrise. Many of the houses that lined the streets were alive with lit lanterns and people preparing for market day.

Simon hurried to move through the crowded streets. His heifer stumbled and mooed at the commotion. All were busy with their own agendas, and no one stopped the wagon for questioning.

The buckboard jostled through the rough streets. George heard Simon hail friendly greetings. He was anxious to stretch his legs and move his stiffened body, but the warnings of the evening prior were fresh on his mind. He remained still and quiet.

Simon pulled his wagon into a bank barn. The door slid closed behind them.

George was relieved to hear the planned series of knocks. His fingers fumbled to open the lock. Tears flooded his eyes when he saw Simon's face. He couldn't speak.

"Quickly, George. Come, quickly." Simon's tone was tense.

George forced his body to move. His legs and feet were completely numb. He collapsed to the floor with a loud thud.

Simon helped him to his feet. He whispered, "Quickly. We have unwanted company."

George struggled to reach the trap door in the floor. His feet shuffled and scraped the wooden floor as it groaned under his weight. He skidded into the opening before he felt his feet. He slid the lock into place.

Two heavy thuds hit the floor above George. With the shuffling of boots and splashing of water, bits of fresh sawdust filtered through the floorboards and coated his throat. He dared not make a sound.

Fists pounded the closed barn door. "Open up! We know you are in there!" The voices grew angrier, more desperate. "I said, open up. NOW!"

Simon and the landowner obeyed the command. Ten men burst through the door. The marshal knocked Simon from his feet. He stood quickly and brushed the dust and damp hay from his pants.

"What is the meaning of this outburst?" accused Enoch, the landowner.

The tall bald marshal moved into his face. He stood eight inches taller than Enoch. His tone was harsh and accusatory.

"Who is this man?" His finger was embedded into Simon's chest.

Simon stepped into his extended hand, forcing the man to remove it from his body. "My name is Simon Tuttle. I am here to sell my heifer at the market auction. We have arrived early and were invited to a bite of breakfast."

"We?" the man sneered.

Innocence flooded from Simon's face. "Yes. My cow, Bessie and I." He chuckled at the men and added, "Is there a problem?"

The rest of the men scattered around the barn. They slid hay bales across the floor, circled the wagon, and jumped on its floor. They searched the perimeter of the barn for anything out of the ordinary, but found nothing.

Enoch grew annoyed at their presence. "State your business!" Only grunts came in reply.

The clang of a bell sounded from the house. A woman's voice rose above the tension, "Breakfast!" The bell continued to ring.

Enoch extended his hand to the man standing before him, "Excuse us, sir, our meal waits." He turned to Simon, "Shall you join me?"

The men finished their inspection of the barn. Satisfied that their Watcher was incorrect and no slave was present, they dismissed themselves, jumped onto their horses, and disappeared down the road. Simon and Enoch walked to the house in silence while George trembled beneath the trap door.

George wiped the tears from his eyes. He knew this journey would be dangerous, but he had miscalculated how closely they were being watched. He whispered a silent prayer of thanksgiving for Simon's guardianship. He allowed his thoughts to turn to Lacey.

After hours of memorizing the names that Lacey circled on the Bugle, he knew he had arrived at the home of Enoch Karn. He was successfully smuggled across the state lines of Georgia and South Carolina and now rested in the center of North Carolina.

Enoch's home was settled on the north end of Doilsburg. It was a large rural community famous for the market. Each month men traveled from the surrounding states to sell their animals and wares. It was the oldest continuous sale in the area and for unknown reasons commanded the highest of market prices. Doilsburg's hub connected many railroad systems to the North and most of the goods sold at the market were shipped to either New York or Boston.

It was a town under close scrutiny for slave smuggling. It was estimated that ten to twelve smuggled slaves passed through each week. Few attempts had been thwarted, making it one of the most successful of its kind. Enoch, with Simon's help, had much to do with that statistic.

George heard the conversation overhead. He recognized Simon's voice and smiled.

"How much do you think she will fetch, Enoch?"

"Oh, I would say you could expect thirty dollars."

"Thirty dollars! That is good news."

The men fed the heifer and filled her water trough again. Simon made a few adjustments on the wagon wheels and retied Bessie to the back.

The men embraced and Simon whispered, "He is in your care now. God be with you — a*lways.*

"And with you," Enoch replied. He watched his friend lead his cow toward the sale.

The Ward plantation woke to the sound of a clanging bell. The sleepy slaves knew this could only mean one thing — someone has escaped. They followed the silent drill and stood in their respective places. Only one spot remained empty.

Samuel burst through the door of George's shack, tearing the door from its flimsy hinge. It wedged in the header denying entrance. Enraged he pounded the wood until only splinters laid at his feet. They echoed an eerie crunch as he stalked the interior. George's name bounced from wall to wall, but no reply came.

Grey ashes lay cold on the ground just beyond George's front step. The letters G-O-R-G-Ǝ stared back at him. Samuel's nostrils flared as he crushed the backwards E.

The manor house door bounced off the wall when Samuel entered the center hall. His word rattled the crystal chandelier. "Camellia!"

His wife tossed her needlepoint to the floor and ran down the center staircase. The look on her husband's face left little doubt.

"He has done it again!"

She stood silently waiting for his rage to subside. Finally she asked, "George?"

He shook his head, "His bed is cold. Judging from the ashes of his last fire, I say he has been gone several days."

"Days?"

"When was the last time you saw him?"

Camellia closed her eyes. She thought about the day her granddaughter came to visit, the look of admiration on his face, the playfulness of his first ice cube. Gruff words stole her memories.

"Damn it, woman! Why are you smiling? We have just lost one of our best!" His words filtered through clenched teeth. "Summon the house staff! If I have to beat the answers out of them, I will!"

From the top of the stairs, Lilly called to her father. "You will do no such thing!" Samuel and Camellia spun to face their daughter. She glared at her father as she sauntered down the stairs.

"Lacey loved George."

"George is gone! Naught can be done to him until I find him!" His anger spun out of control. Each word escalated in pitch until he had to spit them out of his mouth. "He will not survive the tightening of another link. It will choke him!" He lunged at his daughter, "If I don't kill him first!"

Lilly remained steadfast. She had seen too many of these ridiculous outbursts over the years. With hatred etching her face, she slapped her father.

The kitchen staff slid from view at the sound of Camellia's gasp. A crash of a dropped kettle spurred an unnecessary flurry of activity. The resonating ring seemed to escalate the tension.

"Get out of my sight!" Samuel screamed at his daughter.

Lilly never moved. "You disgust me, Father. Get control of yourself, for I am ashamed."

"Ashamed!" he mocked, "You are the one who brings shame on this family. Do you think I do not know? All those years spent in the company of a Negro slave!" He jammed his finger into her chest. "*You* taught him to write, to read…under *my* roof! Me shame you?"

"He is a good man."

"He is *my* man. I own him. I bought and paid for him. I gave him food and a place to lay his head."

"And he gave you work — hard labor. Days and years without complaint. And how did you repay him? By throwing him in the sweat box."

"He tried to flee! I own him. He has no rights!"

"He has served you well, for years."

"And I have taken care of him. I have given him a home."

"You call that miserable shack a home? Scraps for food, dirty water…" Her voice softened, "Father, what has become of you? Where is your compassion? George desires freedom."

"They all desire freedom! But what will become of them? Do you think they could survive on their own, uneducated and backwards? They would not survive. They *need* me!"

"No, Father, you are mistaken. They may not be learned people, but that can be remedied. It is the future. Let them have a choice."

"A choice! They are my property, bought with my blood. They have no choice. They are here to serve." He spun to face Camellia, "What nonsense is this? This is *your* daughter. *You* have allowed these ridiculous notions to grow and become insurmountable." He paced the floor and pulled at his hair. "They are here for one purpose — to serve!"

"Serve whom?" Lilly stepped forward.

"You, your mother, this land. You have forgotten how difficult this world can be. You have lived a charmed life. I have permitted it, and this is how you repay me with sugared words of freedom, the future, and compassion? This talk sickens me."

"It was Lacey's desire." Lilly bit her lip.

The surprise of her statement knocked the anger from her father's words. His response came in a whisper. "What did you say?"

"It was Lacey's last request." Her nails gripped the newel post for support.

Samuel stared at his daughter in disbelief. *Did he understand Lilly correctly? Did Lacey somehow help him escape? But Lacey has been gone too long. George has only been missing a few days. Someone had to help Lacey. She was just a child. She did not have the resources or the vision to help a slave slip out of sight. Someone had to….*

His back stiffened. He clenched his fist. He finally understood. He turned to Camellia, "Remove her from my sight." He dismissed his daughter with a wave of his hand. "He is a dead man!" He stepped into Lilly until his nose nearly touched hers. He tore his lapel from his jacket. With grit, he whispered, "And *you* are dead to me."

20

George spent four days hidden below the floorboards of Enoch's protection. He was given three meals a day and plenty of water to drink, but he never left his cramped hiding place.

Many men passed through Enoch's barn in those four days. Lying on a straw mattress, George listened to their conversations and dreamed of the day he could stand freely among them. They spoke of trains and buckboards, the rising cost of grain, newspapers, and the growing unrest in the South. One conversation was most interesting to George: three men spoke of a bounty.

"I say to you I have never seen Samuel Ward so incensed. He stood on the front porch of the mercantile waving these papers in the air," his words were rushed. "He grabbed my collar and shoved the bounty notice in my hands. *'Return him to me,'* he said with clenched teeth. His mouth foamed like a mad dog!" He handed the crumpled paper to Enoch.

Enoch walked to the edge of the hidden trap door, pretending to need more light to read its contents. He wanted to be sure George heard this conversation, not to cause anxiety but to show the grave necessity of silence and caution. He read the poster aloud:

WANTED
Dead or Alive

A Slave named George
Wearing a tag from Oak Bend
Bearing the marks of prior attempts
$1000 Reward for his return

Master Samuel Ward
Oak Bend, Georgia

Enoch studied the hunger in the men's eyes. Their faces were wild with the idea of capturing the one thousand dollar bounty.

A thin smile spread across his lips. "How does Master Ward expect to catch his slave when there is no image of his likeness? How would one know they have the right man?"

One of the men leaned into Enoch and whispered, "By his own pen we will catch him. His E's are written backwards." Convinced he had the smoking gun he straightened his shoulders, crossed his arms, and nodded his head in affirmation.

Enoch began to laugh. "Forgive me gentleman, but I do not see the validity of a written backwards E as proof. Master Ward needs an image."

"No one has photographs of their property."

"If this slave is so valued to warrant a one thousand dollar reward, I should think Mr. Ward would have him photographed. Otherwise the search is futile."

"But it is one thousand dollars — dead or alive!"

"I do not think a dead slave would be much good to Master Ward." He chuckled, "Gentlemen, I assure you it will be extremely difficult to find this man with this loose description. I am sorry I cannot help you." The floorboard creaked as he walked away from his post.

George swallowed his scream. Although Enoch had performed well in the wake of the anxious men, he knew his troubles had only begun. For the first time he began to doubt his freedom.

His thoughts of dread were broken by the knocks above his head. He slid the lock open. He was greeted by Enoch's grave face and a hot bowl of soup. No words were exchanged; none were needed. George understood.

During his four day stay, twice George had company in his cramped quarters — a young slave from South Carolina and another from Georgia. They did not share their names. It would be safer to keep that hidden.

Both of the men had a different path to take than George. One was taken out the same way George came in; the other left on foot. George knew the peril that awaited them. He blessed them when their time came as they fled under the cover of darkness.

Early in the morning of the fifth day Enoch returned to the barn after transporting the last slave. The horses snorted and pawed at the familiar floor. Light from a lone lantern pierced the dark spaces below. Straw bales slid on the floor above George's head. When the series of planned knocks were finished, George popped his head out of the trap door.

Enoch's face was drawn from sleeplessness. His words were breathless and slow.

"Tonight you will be taken to the train tracks by way of a similar wagon. When the train stops to refuel and pick up passengers, I will be seen filling the cattle cars with fresh hay. You will remain hidden until I say it is time. Quickly you will hide yourself in the center of a hollow bale." He sighed at George's size, "I need not explain that you must fit. You must make yourself fit, George, or all will be lost. When I am loading, the inspectors will come. Often they search, other times they pass without care. They know me for this is my main source of income; yet have no false hope that trust rests in familiarity. They have long suspected my involvement with the cause, but not once have their doubts been proven. Quickly you must hide and remain secreted until the train leaps into action. Do you understand?"

"Yes, sir. I understand."

Enoch pointed to a slightly larger hay bale. "This is the one we will use. Let's fashion this together to ensure your safety."

Together, the two men pulled the hay from the center of the bale. Several times George attempted to crawl inside, but it was too small. After nearly an hour and some extra binder twine, George's hiding place was ready. After loading the majority of the wagon, George slid into the false bottom of the buckboard.

Enoch piled the hay on top of the secret opening with the hollowed bale resting on the top. He whistled to the team of horses and the wagon moved from position. The floorboards groaned under the heavy weight. Within a matter of minutes George was rocked to sleep by its fluid motion.

A starless night hid their intentions. Enoch moved through his familiar path without resistance. He stopped at the first car and filled it with half of his bales.

Carefully he counted the cars until he reached the nineteenth one. His ears were bent for any strange sound. Comfortable that no one was in sight he slid from the seat and opened the door.

Greeted by the familiar scent of fresh dung, he scraped the waste from the entrance. He placed a large bale on the ground to use as a temporary step. Within minutes he shoveled an area clean to stack his bales. He tossed eight oversized bales onto the wooden floor. The ninth one landed a bit softer.

He whistled to George as a signal of free passage. George jumped from the wagon and hid himself into the hollowed bale. Enoch loaded the balance of his hay into the rail car. He opened the last two bales and spread their contents over the newly cleaned floor. He filled the troughs for the cattle and jumped from the train.

He tossed the last bale onto the floor at the entrance of the door. This was another unspoken symbol of a hidden slave to the next group of Abolitionists. Just before he closed the door, he started to sing. George smiled, for he knew his friend was saying goodbye.

With a burst of pressure the brakes unlocked, and the train began to move down the tracks. George whispered, "I, George, am free from slavery."

Simon crumpled his paperwork and shoved it into his pocket. The auctioneer rambled as he took his place near the back of the crowd. He recognized a few faces from his fiery encounter but looked through them. Their searing eyes burned his skin. He moved toward the front to avoid their stares.

"Going once...twice...sold for $28.10."

Simon shook his head at the price. She was a good cow and showed great promise of a good milk producer, but she did look a bit haggard from her road trip. He stood in line for his payment.

Two men flanked him and squeezed his body in the middle. Simon muscled his way out of their silent oppression.

"Can I help you, gentlemen?"

"We're watching you, Simon Tuttle," scoffed the man on his left.

With one more shove the men disappeared into the crowd. Simon pocketed his heifer money and quickly walked to his wagon. Once away from the dark stares he began to relax. He had a long, lonely ride home.

People from the sale filled the streets. Simon passed the family that bought his heifer. He tipped his hat and waved as he rode by. Once outside of the city limits the foot traffic lightened and within an hour Simon was the only wagon on the road.

He hummed and sang to pass the time. Red, pink, and purple hues lit the sky with a brilliant sunset as his wagon wheels continued to roll. He did not stop the first night for sleep. He wanted to put some distance between himself and the shadowed eyes of his oppressors. He shook his head to clear their faces from his thoughts.

Without his heifer in tow Simon made good time. By morning he was only one-half day's ride from the edge of his friend's plantation. He tried to convince his body to relax, yet he had a constant feeling of dread that would not yield.

Throughout the morning he felt watched. In his peripheral vision he caught glimpses of movement along the edge of the road, but when he turned to look he saw only trees and scrub brush. After the third instance he cracked his whip. The horses reared and jumped into action. The wagon jarred along the rough road. Simon bit his lip twice from the jolt.

The team finally broke through the cover of the woods into a wide-open plain. The road was littered with washed out ruts and made a quick getaway impossible without being tossed from the seat.

He pulled the horses' reins. "Whoa, boys. That was a tough ride, but...."

Without warning a man jumped into the back of his buckboard. He rushed toward Simon wielding a knife. The men fell to the ground. Simon tried to protect himself from his assailant, but he was badly wounded.

He felt the hot blade pierce his lung. His left arm hung limp at his side. The man overpowered him and sat on his chest. Simon struggled to breathe.

From the corner of his eye Simon saw flying flames as torches were thrown onto his buckboard. The remnants of straw quickly caught. The horses panicked and forced the fiery wagon to flip on its side. They ran through the open field until they were seen no more. Simon was left alone with a band of thugs.

"Watch him burn," the man taunted. His blade was pressed hard against Simon's throat.

"Who burn?" Simon finally managed to whisper.

"The slave you have hidden in your wagon, Mr. Tuttle."

The fact that these men knew his name unnerved Simon, but he fought hard to breathe and keep his composure.

"I know not of what you are speaking. I have no slave in my wagon." The pain in his lung, coupled with the weight of the man sitting on his chest made Simon's head swoon. His world started to spin, his words were reduced to babbling, and he struggled for air.

Blood trickled from his mouth. He felt his lungs fill with warm fluid. His vision narrowed. All color was removed from his sight. A bright light appeared over him. He reached his right arm toward it and felt his body lifted. His head hit the road with a soft thud.

The man climbed off Simon's chest. He looked in the direction that Simon was reaching for — nothing was there. The rest of the men gathered around the fire. They taunted and sneered as the flames grew higher and wilder. They danced and laughed like drunken men.

"One more gone!" one man shouted. Cheers came from the crowd.

"To the success of another slave returned to the dust from which he came!"

"Meet your maker!" shouted another.

The man who had killed Simon Tuttle joined the frenzied group. His words held the tone of disgust. "You best be putting out that fire to gather that slave's bones. We must have something to show for the bounty!"

The men gathered what water they had available and added the dry earth to quench the fire's thirst. They pulled the wagon apart and stomped the flames into submission. When they inspected the ashes, no bones were found.

"This wagon was empty, sir! No slave in here."

The group stared at the smoldering wood. Bits of black charred remains beset the idle field. The men looked at the limp body splayed on the road. Not a word was spoken. They had killed without cause.

The leader slammed his boot into the smoking ground. "His wagon may be empty this time, but innocent he is not!" He waved his hand toward the edge of the field, "Gather his horses. They are our spoil." He whistled to his own, jumped on his back, and disappeared from where he came.

The men did as they were told and tried to gather Simon's horses. One refused to be caught and reared in defiance. His hooves cut the man's face and forced his body to the ground. The horse disappeared into the open field. The men did not follow him. They rode in silent fear back to their homes aware of the damage they had inflicted.

Mary Tuttle waited anxiously for her husband's return. He was a day overdue, and she could not shake the hollow feeling.

On the second day one of Simon's horses came alone. His mane and tail were singed and his hind legs were covered with lacerations. She collapsed to the ground. Her children gathered around to comfort and to share in her grief.

The following day, her eldest son of fifteen placed a second blue bonnet beside the faded one.

"I cannot continue without your father."

"Do you believe in the cause, Mother?"

"You know I do."

"Then, we must continue. It is what Father would have wanted."

"I do not have the strength, or desire."

"You may not, but I do."

"No, I will not allow it."

"Mother, I am filled with anger and sadness. I should have gone with him. Although we have not yet received word, we know his fate. I cannot allow his commitment to die with him. We must continue. These people do not have a voice. Without us, they may not have hope." He lowered his head and eyes in submission. "Mother, I am asking for your blessing." He took her hand, "Please, Mother."

Tears moistened her face. She made no attempt to dry them. It was necessary to permit them to flow.

"My dear son, this business is a grave one." Her voice quivered, "Others are committed to the cause. They can continue without us."

Their conversation was interrupted by the sound of horse hooves. From over the hill two men on horseback approached them; the third drove a wagon. Mary grabbed her son's arm.

"Mary," the man spoke softly. "We are so sorry for your loss." He helped her to the wagon where Simon's body was settled into a coffin. She wept again.

"I knew this was his fate. My heart told me so." She struggled to keep her voice steady.

The man explained all he knew of Simon's death. He spared her the details of the position of his body. Mary listened without a sound but not without tears. When he finished speaking, he gave her a piece of paper.

"When we found him, this was in his hand."

She opened up the crumpled bloodstained parchment. It held only one word written by Simon's hand. It read:

Always

Mary brought the paper to her chest and sobbed. She knew what it meant. She knew it was his message to her — a pledge of his unfailing love and unwavering belief in the cause of freedom. She thanked the men for returning Simon to the family. They buried him on the west hill overlooking the farm.

"Here, he will be able to watch over us. We will gather our strength from his example and love." She turned to her eldest son, "Tonight, we will light a candle in the second window."

22

Georg woke to the sound of squealing brakes. The train jerked to a sudden stop. Within moments voices were heard approaching his car. He climbed inside his hollow bale and covered his head just as the door flung open. Daylight lit the car, and through the many gaps in his hand-fashioned hiding place, it pierced his eyes. A lump formed in his throat. He prayed he was covered.

Their feet shuffled across the wooden floor. They thrust long knives into several of the bales. George held his breath as they walked around the pile of hay.

"Nothing in here," one man said as he jumped from the open doorway.

The men left as quickly as they came. The door flew shut. The clang resonated throughout the railcar. George listened as they repeated the process down the tracks. He was about to breathe for the first time when he heard a loud scream in the distance.

The earth rattled from the pounding of many feet as they rushed passed George's car to help. From the sounds of the screams and the language he heard, it left little doubt that the men had found what they were looking for — a slave.

George listened as they questioned the slave. He heard the cracks of the whips and loud whimpers pleading them to stop. If he could've covered his ears, he would have done it, but the bale left no room for movement.

Finally, with the shout of the plantation's name, the cries lessened. The men whipped the slave several more times, and then came the jingle of the shackles. George knew that sound well. It was the sound of slavery. He wept for his comrade though he knew not his name.

Soon the train began to move and fall into its normal rhythm. Yet even with the fluid movement, George's nerves choked his relief. He felt strangled by the dried hay. He pushed his way out of the bale and struggled to catch his breath. With his second step his face crashed to the floor with a thud. A moan pierced the darkness.

George's eyes opened wide, "Who's there?" Only the sound of shuffling could be heard. George spoke more sternly, "I said, who's there?"

"Jus me, suh. Jus me." The man's voice was timid.

"Who's me?"

"Monroe, suh. My name's Monroe."

"Where did you come from?" George slowly approached the sound of the voice. He could identify the man by his dialect.

"I followed those men back there. Knew they was huntin' slaves. I kept mysuf hid and made the move jus 'for they shut the doh."

"Where are you from?"

"Africa."

"No, where is your master?"

"Oh suh, don't takes me back there. Please, my massa's a bad man. He was fixin' to send me off to Otta

Island `for I `scaped." He started to cry, "Theys die there, suh, on Otta Island."

George knelt beside Monroe. With his eyes adjusting to the dim light, he saw the man was missing his left hand. The wound was not recent.

"What happened to your hand, Monroe?"

"My massa cuts it off. He caught me stealin'. I'sa jus hungry. Tooks a chicken." His face lit from the memory. "Was a mighty fine tastin' chicken. I cooked it mysuf. Ate it all `for I got kot." He frowned, "Massa said he done teach me a lesson not to steal no chicken again." Silent tears dripped off his face and dampened his tattered shirt, "He's a bad man, my massa."

"Was anyone helping you escape?"

"No, suh."

"You followed those men alone?" George questioned.

"I says no one's helpin' me. I never says I's alone."

George heard shuffling just beyond the hay bales. A thin figure moved into the center of the railcar. It was a woman.

Monroe whispered, "This is my sista, Mim...or a...Myra."

The woman moved into the passing light of the rail car slats. She stood proud, yet her face was down turned. She wore a weathered straw hat, a cotton calico dress, and only one shoe.

Her light blue eyes sparkled as she walked to George. She extended her hand to him. "I am pleased to make your acquaintance. Please call me Mim; `twas a nickname given to me by my brother when he was just a young boy."

George was struck by her poise. Her speech was much different than that of Monroe's. Her skin was the color of coffee mixed with cream. She was lean but toned. Her hair

117

was long, wavy, and chestnut brown, but in her eyes there was little doubt that she was a mixed breed. George thought she was beautiful.

He took her hand and smiled, "George. My name is George."

23

In the summer of 1860, Rebecca rode to Salem alone. She wore the pain of her absent mother like a badge of honor. She was determined to carry on the family business. Not many suspected her involvement in the cause. Her subtleties in gathering information were well orchestrated and nearly invisible. Her mother had taught her well.

She saw Daniel Hise approaching from a distance. His carriage of choice was his own feet. He preferred walking to riding unless speed was a necessity. He brushed past Rebecca without a glance, smile, or word. She gathered the small piece of paper in her glove and tucked it into her corset a few paces later.

Her first stop was the mercantile. The glances and whispers of the patrons in the building were always the same, for the owner was one of Hanna's Watchers. Although that was unknown to Rebecca, her level of comfort in the shop was minimal. She felt their eyes while they scrutinized and calculated. Once she finished her purchases, she walked outside to breathe the free air.

"I shudder at that place," she whispered under her breath. "But it is a necessary evil."

She walked a few more blocks to the cobbler to pick up a pair of her father's boots that were in bad need of repair.

"We offer our condolences to you and your father, Rebecca. Your mother was a grand lady."

Rebecca struggled not to release her emotions. It had been only two months since her mother's murder, and each visit to Salem held the same result.

Her face revealed her sadness, yet she managed a smile. "Thank you, Mr. Hiram. I miss her more than words." Her hands brushed the pleats in her skirt. When she gained her composure she asked, "What is the charge for the repair?"

Mr. Hiram removed his eyeglasses and wiped the lenses with a soft cloth. His moist breath fogged the glass, and he repeated the process until both lenses were free of smudges.

Rebecca in her impatience spoke, "Mr. Hiram, if you please, the cost?"

He chuckled at her eagerness. "There is no charge for you today, Miss Rebecca. Consider it Mrs. Hiram's way of extending a hand."

"Why, that is very kind of you both. Thank you."

He tipped his hat and stared at her over his clean spectacles. She felt a cold chill as she left his shop, though she did not know why.

Her last stop was for pleasure. She slipped into the confectionary. She rocked on her heels as her eyes moved through the delicacies. She spied a cluster of sugar sticks tinted pink, green, and yellow. She asked for a yellow one and refused the paper sack. Her giggle revealed her true age. She slipped off her glove, peeled away the paper, and finished the maple sugar treat before she stepped onto her wagon.

She arrived in time to see the young man of the mercantile throw the last feed sack onto the back of her wagon. With it fully loaded with a week's supplies, she slipped off her other white glove and rode toward home.

The afternoon sun was high. She pulled her bonnet to shade her face from its searing rays. The air was still – no breeze or birds dared to fly.

Tired of the sun, she moved the horses through an unmarked path that cut through a virgin forest. The Osage orange trees stood like sentries at its entrance. Their thorned branches pulled at her clothing as she drove through the narrow opening.

The slack in the reins drooped onto her boots. The horses needed no guidance, for they knew the path well. Soon the wagon rested in the center of an open glen.

Sunlight filtered through the low maple branches dappling the ground with sunspots. Rebecca slid from the seat and walked to the center of the clearing. She pulled the snippet of paper from her corset.

The birds announced her arrival. Without so much as a rustle of a leaf, four men surrounded her and supported their weight on Daniel's hand-forged rods. She approached one of them and held out the paper. He nodded his head as he took it from her and passed it to the man on his right. One by one, all of the men read the message, but no one spoke.

Nathaniel was the last to read the note. He lit a match and watched the numbers 1 — 19 — 3 disappear from the flaming message that floated on the breeze. The group slipped their rods under their black cloaks and disappeared into the thicket that surrounded the clearing. Once the sounds of the horses' hooves were silent Rebecca gathered the charred remains. The fragment disintegrated in her hands. She blew the dust from her fingers and wiped the black stain onto the damp moss.

With the numbers on the paper seared into the Abolitionists' minds, the plan was set in motion. The first number signaled the number of slaves; the second was the specific railcar that the slave is hidden; the last number revealed all would take place on the third train the following day.

Nathaniel's role was carried out in apt precision. He and one other rode that evening to place the rods by the side door of the summoned. Tomorrow evening the men would gather and ride to the train stop on the west side of Salem. In the nineteenth car a single slave would be found and smuggled to his next safe house.

24

When the train pulled away from the station, George knew the next stop would be his last. Long stares replaced conversation. With each rattle and sway of movement every breath seemed more labored and less frequent. George tried to soothe his nerves by turning his thoughts to his journey through the help of Lilly and Lacey. They came in rhythm.

> *My thoughts of home are clouded,*
> *Hazy and long beyond*
> *The swagger of the train*
> *That echoes the ship,*
> *Which left my dreams adrift.*
>
> *Years of toil shade the laughter*
> *Of my meager existence.*
> *Smiles turn to frowns and tears to cries*
> *And are muffled by blurred moments*
> *Of hollowed eyes.*

The spoiled choke of freedom
That crushes my thoughts,
And restricts my lungs
Are disguised as a necklace.
Only the tag swings free.

If only I could allow
A moment of peace to dream
Of air that is free,
And easy to breathe,
I would be able to christen it as mine.

Who would believe
That hope would come
In the form of a child
Radiant with life,
Staging a flower for a name?

Her frail eyes held passion,
Joy and an unwavering will
To see an injustice loosened,
Sanctioned and polished,
With my liberty as the prize.

To a weary man she granted a wish,
One he could not grasp
Or will by his own hand.
A graceful Lilly, who gave birth to Lacey,
That restored my deep desires.

She spoke with wisdom,
Knowledge and independence

With a pen and paper.
A simple scheme in a box
With coins and a watch, sprung by a key.

I hold her memory
Of beauty and life
In the form of her name,
Embroidered and edged
With her pure heart.

To you, little Lacey
And to you, dear Lilly,
My mind often wanders
And envisions your smiles.
With me, I carry your dreams.

For by your will I am here,
And by your love I have strength.
For without you my chosen words
Could not be spoken:
I, George, am free from slavery.

The train whistle sounded its arrival. It was nine-thirty in Salem, Ohio, and in the nineteenth rail car George forced his body into the hollowed bale for the final time after settling his two new friends into their own bales. An unwavering smile covered his face.

25

The sound of the train's arrival summoned the attention of Nathaniel's men. As often as this ritual occurred, no freedom call was ever easy. Nathaniel covered his heart with his hand to silence its rapid movement.

The engine rounded the familiar bend. Soon the train slowed to a stop. The rush of steam pierced the night air with anticipation.

Monroe, Mim, and George remained hidden until the sound of releasing coal rattled through the cars. Under its cover, the door was forced open. Rebecca was the voice of the freedom call.

"Fly," she spoke in whispered haste.

To the band's surprise, three slaves jumped from the train. Questions covered the men's faces, yet no words were uttered. There was no time for hesitation.

George was ushered to a false-bottom buckboard. Nathaniel jumped onto the seat and moved the horses into a gait without a command. Rebecca followed closely behind on her unsaddled mare.

The other two men took Monroe and Mim in opposite directions. Only one man stayed behind to close the door with the final dump of coal. A pile of stones, a bottle of whiskey, and a well-rehearsed cover lingered in his mind.

He held the cold metal door inches from closing. Only a hard shove would hold it in place once the lock was broken. He held his breath and listened for his cue. It seemed an eternity until the trickle of the coal could be heard dropping from above. When the sound was at its peak, he slammed the door closed. Voices approached from the opposing side of the train.

His horse galloped down the hardened path with only one foot secured in the stirrups. He swung his body over the moving saddle and settled into familiarity. His intentions disappeared with him into the shadows. The voices vanished with the growing distance between them.

Rebecca rode with her father to Unserheim, and to the security of Daniel and Margaret Hise. It was the first time Nathaniel permitted his daughter to accompany the group. It was against his better judgment, but he could not resist Rebecca's consistent pleading despite the memory of Abigail's warning.

It was a cloudy, moonless night. The houses were dark and still as Nathaniel and Rebecca crept by unnoticed. Even the horses' hooves were silent. The lone lantern lit inside Daniel's barn was a welcomed sight.

The thump of the anvil bounced through the room with each strike of Daniel's hammer. His back was set toward the sliding door, and he did not turn when Nathaniel led the horses and wagon into its safety. Rebecca slid from her mare and closed the door behind them.

"How goes the ride?" Daniel asked as he submerged the hot metal into a bath of cool water.

Nathaniel's response, "Without difficulty," was smothered by the swish and spit of the water's steam.

Daniel turned to face his friend and settled his eyes on Rebecca. He smiled.

"Unable to sleep?"

"I cannot sit idly by."

He patted her shoulder but spoke not his mind. He felt it too dangerous for a young woman. Her task of information gathering and distributing was perilous enough; her mother's loss of life resonated that reminder.

Nathaniel studied the expressions on his dear friend's face. He understood his wrestling thoughts and thought it best to calm his doubts.

"Her insistence was impossible to thwart. She is aware this is her sole ride." He smiled at his daughter, "She will not ask again."

Rebecca hung her head in shame. Daniel lifted it gently. His eyes were flooded with softness.

"Take no shame in your convictions. We are answering to The Almighty for the work we are called to do. Each of us believes that slavery is an abomination as we continue to encourage our President to proclaim emancipation for our brethren. They are born into the color of the skin by the master design of God. It is a sin to enter into the empire of slavery. It is not in our government's best interest to condone that behavior, much less perpetuate it for profit."

He walked to the wagon, pulled the straw bales away from the hidden door, and knocked. The sound of the bolt sliding open had the musicality of liberty to all in the room.

Daniel extended his hand to the slave, "Welcome! Welcome to the protection I can give, with or without the law!"

Daniel's red hair and beard seemed to be the source of the light that dimly lit the interior of the barn. The men shook hands, and Daniel quickly guided George into a trap door in the floor.

"Quietly now, follow the tunnel until you reach its end. A warmer greeting will be yours after you find the burning lantern."

Daniel closed the trap door and tossed a few forks of straw on the floor to conceal its seams. He led Nathaniel and Rebecca down the flagstone walkway and through the east center door of Unserheim.

George found himself in a dark, narrow tunnel that disappeared through the wall of the bank barn. He lit the candle stub Daniel had given to him moments before he closed the door. The sound of their footsteps moved farther from him until the passageway was eerily silent. He lifted the candle into the air and started to crawl.

The tunnel walls and ceiling were formed of handmade bricks. The opening was barely three feet round and George struggled to move his body through. He noticed a few markings scratched into the surface of the bricks. The fresh symbols stood out as brilliant white against the dark red background. Some were three initials, some only one, but most of the signs were a simple X.

George made his way through a long corridor until the tunnel took a sharp left turn. After a few more feet he saw a faint yellow glow. With every lunge forward the light became brighter, more pronounced, until he made the final bend to the left.

He blew the candle stub out before it burned his fingers. A small wooden butter bowl held remnants of many similar freedom crawls. George tossed his stub into the bowl and continued to work his way toward the lantern.

When he pulled his body through the last of the brick channel, it opened into a stonewalled room nearly eight feet wide and ten feet long. On a corner table sat a pitcher of cool water and an empty glass beside the illuminated lantern. George ignored the glass and drank straight from the pitcher until it was empty.

On the opposite wall sat a hired-man's rope bed. Its low stance forced George's knees nearly to his chest, but the position was a welcome change from the weeks of flight. He rubbed the thighs of his soiled pants.

He heard footsteps overhead on the wooden ceiling. He blew out the flame of the lantern and moved his body back into the entrance of the tunnel. A voice called to him from the opening. He recognized the gentle voice as Daniel's.

"Come."

George popped out of the trap door opening in the floor of the rear entry. The room burst into laughter. Rebecca pulled the remnants of straw from his hair. She could not remove her eyes from the tortuous mark imbedded into his neck, and he could not turn away from the color of her golden hair.

"My name is George."

"Rebecca," she replied while holding her index finger to her chest. She extended her hand to her father and Daniel and introduced them.

"Where is your home, George?" Daniel's voice was soft and filled with concern.

"My master is from Oak Bend in Georgia, but Africa, sir, is my home."

"Africa was your birthplace?"

"Yes, sir. I was taken from her shores as a young boy. I have been in Georgia ever since."

"Have you given much thought to your next plan?" Nathaniel's words pierced George's thoughts.

"No, sir," he hung his head.

Daniel gripped George's shoulders, "We have much time for that discussion, my friend, but for tonight, you are safe. Come, eat, and rest. Sleep will come easy."

Margaret had prepared a pot of beef stew. The aroma permeated the kitchen and adjacent entry. The dining room curtains were drawn leaving the room dimly lit by a lone oil lamp. George sat at the seat of honor for the second time in his life. He placed Lacey's box on the table.

Rebecca's curiosity ensued, "What is of the wooden box, George?"

Tears filled his eyes. "It is a simple box of memories."

"A memory box?" she asked.

"This is not my first attempt to flee my master, yet this is the farthest north I have been; thanks in part by this box, but mostly to a young girl named Lacey."

George spoke of Lilly and Lacey through three bowls of stew. His animated face carried the abolitionists through his tale of escape, capture, and torture. He explained how Lacey abetted his dream and gave him the tools for a successful attempt. He opened the box.

"This was the first newspaper I have read." He held up the well-used copy of The Anti-Slavery Bugle.

Margaret gasped. George was unaware of the significance of the newspaper. From reading its contents, he knew it was published and printed in Salem but did not give much regard to how Lacey, a young girl of Georgia, would come to possess a copy. He continued with his story.

"Lacey made me memorize the names she circled. She numbered each one in order that I should find them." He pointed to the two names of the men who helped him on this journey and explained all that had happened to him in the past few weeks. His eyes fell on the last name. His hand shook as he rested his finger under the third and final name that Lacey had marked.

"And this one, sir," he turned to Nathaniel, "is the last name she gave me."

Nathaniel stared at his name in disbelief. The Bugle's account of his wife's death filled the column. The mention of Abigail's suffering was too much for him to read again. Silent streams seeped from his eyes. He made no move to hide his emotions. Rebecca excused herself from the table.

"I mean you no disrespect, sir."

"None taken, George."

"Your grief is covered by my shame."

Nathaniel managed a smile, "She was a good woman. She believed in the cause as much as we do. To continue in her honor is the least we must do."

Silence from the table grew uncomfortable until a loud pounding came on the south door.

"Daniel!" Margaret's voice was hushed yet urgent.

There was no time to safely take George to the underground tunnel. His only hope of refuge was upstairs. Margaret led George up the back kitchen staircase and through the narrow door that led to the attic. With quick instructions, she ran back down and settled into a chair in the sitting room. Nathaniel sat beside her, and Rebecca was crossed-legged on the floor at her father's feet.

In the landing of the attic staircase was a four-paned window resting at shoulder height. Most walked past the shaded opening without notice. George opened the window and crawled through it. He continued along the wall as directed.

He crawled under a staircase that led to the roof. He slid each floorboard out from underneath their hiding place under the wall's baseboard. Once he transferred his body weight onto the next board, he returned the previous one to its original space until he made his way through the opening into a hidden room. The back roofline concealed the area. It was a large room that could easily hide thirty people without any knowledge of their presence. He pressed his body along the back wall.

Loud muffled voices came from the floor below. George held his breath and tried to discern the words. The northern breeze tossed the lower branches of the maple tree across the slate roof. The scratching sound drowned out all others. George stood alone in the silence praying for his deliverance.

"I, George, want to be free," he whispered to the shadows. "I am tired." He hung his head. "So very tired."

Light pierced the darkness from the opened window. George pressed his body firm against the angled roofline, but he remained hidden from the searching light.

Rebecca's voice whispered, "George? Are you in here?"

"Yes Ma'am." He poked his head out through the opening that sheltered his body. "Are they gone?"

"Yes. It is safe to come out now. There is someone here you will be surprised to see."

George swallowed hard. His face paled to grey.

Rebecca read his anxious thoughts and laughed, "It is Mim. She will be staying this evening as well."

Rebecca explained the inner ways of the freedom fighters as they walked down the two flights of stairs to rejoin the others in the front sitting room. George greeted Mim with a warm hug and settled into the settee beside her.

Their parlor conversation lasted for nearly an hour. George and Mim listened to Daniel as he answered many of their questions. His words and knowledge gave them comfort and hope.

After a moment of reflecting on Daniel's thoughts, George asked, "Am I safe here?"

"George, you must understand that Ohio is considered a free state. Georgia and the Carolinas are slave states, which is why you could not remain. If you had been found, you would have been returned to Master Ward at Oak Bend and suffered the punishment that awaited your return.

"Ohio was different until the passing of the Fugitive Slave Law of 1850. Since its acceptance any slaves in Ohio can be pursued, captured, and returned to their slave masters. Any marshals or others so named as their accomplices that refuse a slave's capture are fined one thousand dollars. The Slave Catchers and Slave Holders are paid a considerable bounty for a slave's return. Even though Ohio remains a free state, one that does not condone or promote slavery, eventual capture is certain if a slave is not hidden."

George instinctively covered his neck with his hands. "I would not have survived another link." He shook his head in memory, "It nearly choked my life from the last reduction."

"Is that why your scar is so deep?" Rebecca timidly asked.

"Yes, Ma'am. My skin grew over the chain. Its tightness stole my comfort," he lowered his voice, "well, of many things."

Rebecca looked at her father. "No man should suffer this injustice."

The men nodded in response though no one spoke.

134

26

GEORGE

Sleep came easy for the first time in weeks. George slept on a soft straw mattress covered with a down feather tick. His body sank into its softness without pause. He dreamed he was floating.

He slept in the winter bedroom addition that Daniel had finished the prior season. After a brutally cold winter Daniel and Margaret decided a warmer bedroom had to be fashioned with an adequate fireplace. It needed to be large enough for the entire family to sleep in case of frigid temperatures. The addition boasted two beds mostly used for Daniel and Margaret and their daughters, Nora and Sis, but it also held many boarders and runaway slaves.

This evening, Mim curled into a tight ball on the smaller bed beside George. She slept with ease. With no need for a fire, the silence added to the comfort.

In the moments just before dawn, fists pounded again on the south door. This act was not uncommon, for it was the door designated for traveling slaves. The slaves were ushered in and asked to wait in the small windowless room to the left until Daniel came to greet them. On this night, the unrelenting thumping left no doubt that this visit was not a slave.

George woke to Nathaniel's hushed voice. "We are under siege! You must hide!"

Nathaniel moved a poplar step-back cupboard and exposed a recessed door only five feet tall. He whispered hurried instruction to George and slid the cupboard into place He play-acted his sleepy entrance while Daniel distracted the men with questions.

Rebecca slid the wool rug from the trap door. Mim jumped into the stone room that George had been in earlier. It was dark and damp, but it was safe.

"Be still and hidden in the entrance of the tunnel. They will not find you."

She closed the door, slid the rug over it, and ran into their bedroom. She straightened the beds as if none had slept beneath their covers. Her feet carried her silently up the back staircase and down the hall to the front bedroom.

Nathaniel questioned his judgment to involve his daughter in this business as he entered the front room. He silently made a promise this was the one and only time.

Four men who accompanied a marshal brushed passed Nathaniel as he entered the room. Daniel held up his hands to silence his friend. His voice was calm and unconcerned. He had much practice. He called to Nathaniel.

"These men think we are harboring a slave." He laughed. "Show them around, my friend, while I wake Margaret."

"No, Daniel," one of the men hissed. "You will accompany us with the search."

"Gentlemen, I assure you this search is futile. You have disturbed the peaceful sleep of my company for what — to satisfy your ridiculous accusations? Please leave us in peace."

"Not until every corner has been searched."

"So be it then." Daniel waved his hand of permission.

The conversation had given George just enough time to run down the basement stairs and slip through another opening. He groped through the darkness of the crawl space until his hand rested on a large boulder. As instructed, he slid around the backside of the foundation stone and entered an opening under the porch. His face stopped inches from exposure. He smelled the fresh dirt and grass of the lawn. The men's shouts were escalated from inside the house. He swallowed hard and prayed for Mim's safety.

It was Daniel's intention when Unserheim was built to incorporate a maze of escape routes. The house had a labyrinth of tunnels and connecting passageways, staircases that led to hidden doorways, trap doors to underground tunnels, or hatches that opened onto the roof which featured three Gothic peaks. Many slaves hid by molding their bodies into the roof pitch making it impossible to be seen from the ground or the hatch.

The house was built with an exhausting number of doors, halls, and windows, which made it virtually impossible to search all corners of the structure. To the aggressors the house appeared smaller – pathways in the attic seemed to end when in reality a room existed just out of view, closets appeared to be shallow when they were actually connected to one another, rooms existed behind obscured windows, and the foundation crawl space had a multitude of hidden exits. The house design was brilliant and served a greater purpose for the lives of the oppressed.

George held his breath as he watched the sun rise. At least an hour had passed before he heard the men's footsteps on the porch floor over his head. He watched as they untied their horses from the rings in the front stone wall and disappeared down Franklin Road.

Nathaniel walked onto the front porch whistling. He sang a little tune signaling to George it was safe for him to come back into the house the way he came. Nathaniel slid the poplar cupboard from the covered door. He greeted the muddy George with a robust laugh and long hug.

He led him into the kitchen where Margaret had prepared a tub with hot water. She poured the last of the steaming water into the galvanized container when he entered the room. They left George to cleanse his body of the morning's events.

George smelled the aroma of sizzling bacon and washed as quickly as possible. After using a razor to rid his face of his beard, he slipped into the clean clothes folded on a chair. He felt like a new man when he entered the kitchen.

All eyes were on him as he sat at the table, especially Mim's. He asked if he could say grace for his food, his new friends, and mostly his freedom. He finished his prayer with a single promise – *always*.

27

After a brief stay at Unserheim, George remained under the care of Nathaniel and Rebecca at their farm. He was shown the passageways and hiding places but never needed to use them. Rebecca had become a remarkable cook and kept the men filled with breakfast and dinner. Lunch was usually a few morsels saved from the previous day's evening meal.

George proved useful around the Kristol farm. His way with the farm animals and hand tools cut Nathaniel's work in more than half.

Rebecca and George became fast friends. She helped George expand his vocabulary and grow in comfort with the scripted word in exchange for stories of Lacey, Lilly, and the South. Nathaniel was grateful for another guardian willing to keep Rebecca within sight, and George was content with his trust.

It was time for Rebecca's weekly ride into town for supplies, but mostly for word of any slaves en route. George was overcome with desire to ride with her, yet he knew he could not.

"You be careful, Miss Rebecca," he warned as he tightened the horse's harness.

"I am always careful, George."

He watched the wagon bounce along the path until it disappeared over a knoll. Nathaniel stood beside him and waved to his daughter. His heart was uneasy.

28

The Ward plantation was in turmoil. A flurry of activity was set in the kitchen. Hot water slopped throughout the room continued its trail up the grand staircase and down the hall to a heavily carved door at its end.

The hinges moaned from overuse. Wool blankets and coverlets were tossed about the room. Slop jars of blood and spew filled the air with a foul, acrid odor. The curtains were drawn to warn the sunshine against its welcome.

Samuel Ward lay prostrate covered with sweat-soaked blankets. His wife Camellia patted his forehead with a cool damp cloth. Lilly stood at the foot of his bed unmoved. The house slaves slid in and out of view without a word or sound. They carried water, hot and cold, to Master Ward's bedside and retreated with the soiled slop jars. The exchange of fresh and foul was constant.

Samuel's skin was an odd shade of translucent grey. The wrinkles around his mouth mimicked the deep concern of the women in the room. His only sound was a constant moan.

141

"When will the doctor arrive?" Lilly's concern broke the deafening silence.

"Not soon enough." Camellia's gaze met Lilly's. "I fear the worst."

"Do not speak those words, Mother. We must secure good thoughts."

"My fear is not only for what is before us, but of what will come." Her lace collar hung limp from long spent tears.

"The doctor, Madam Ward." The slave's eyes lowered as she extended her hand to present the physician.

He took Lilly's hand and nodded. "Miss Lilly."

After a similar greeting to Lady Ward, he opened his black satchel. The women excused themselves from the room. Camellia collapsed into the settee that graced the wide hallway and wept openly. Lilly sat beside her without speaking. Her mind was bent on the task set before her. Three chimes echoed from the tall case clock. The women stared at its hands. By three-fifteen the doctor knelt at their feet. His eyes were grave as he shook his head.

He took Camellia's hand for the second time. "He is calling for you."

She rose with the dignified strength of a true Southern woman. The soft swish of her long skirt disappeared through the doorway. A low muffled conversation filled the room.

"Be strong, Samuel Ward," she spoke through a forced smile with red-rimmed eyes. "There is much to tend to." She held his clammy hand.

Samuel opened his mouth to speak. With each drawn breath only the release of a blood-spattering cough was heard. Camellia tried to calm him, but his persistence was undaunted. Finally he was able to utter one question.

"George?"

Camellia was stunned. Her thoughts were scrambled by his tone. He sounded anxious or angry. She leaned close to his face and stroked his forehead.

"George has yet to be found. Please rest, Samuel. Do not concern yourself with such frivolity. I am not concerned with a slave named George. He has chosen to be forgotten. He left us when our need was great." Her tone escalated with each sentence. "He made a conscious choice. You have wasted enough time, money, and energy on his bounty." She finished her speech with a snap.

"George."

"Shhh, please try to find comfort, Samuel. His name is not worth our lives. Rest my dear husband. Rest."

Samuel became agitated. A violent cough fought his desire to speak. His body thrashed as he struggled to breathe. Camellia stood in horror. The doctor rushed to his bed and forced Samuel's arms to his side. He was unable to calm his convulsions. Lilly turned from the footboard.

With Samuel's last exhale came the word, "...*Free*."

Camellia jumped as if she had been shocked. The doctor mirrored her surprise. Only Lilly smiled; for crumpled in her father's hand was the bounty money she had paid for George's freedom. A single tear slid from the corner of her eye.

In her mind she played the sound of George's voice sitting with Lacey on their final visit, "I, George, am free from slavery."

Tuesday morning's sunrise came and went as normal. The shopkeepers arrived one by one, leading their horses to drink at the fountain at the intersection of Main Street and Broadway. A few proprietors lingered procrastinating the beginning of their day, while others hurried along to take advantage of the early customers in town. After a hectic Monday of playing catch up for a well-deserved day off, Tuesday was usually the most sleepy morning of the week, but not today.

When Jesal Hiram, one of Hanna's Watchers, rode into town, dust was thick from pawing horses. A band of Slave Holders had arrived. Their accusations outnumbered their questions, and within an hour they had rounded up all of the slaves they were searching for, all but one named simply George.

Jesal was quick to pull one of the men into his cobbler shop. With his wife on the lookout for any unwanted ears, he was quick to deliver George's whereabouts. Three men saddled immediately and rode toward Unserheim.

George had arrived to work with Daniel before sunrise. He usually worked for Daniel every Tuesday if he was not needed at the Kristol homestead. This Tuesday was no exception.

Daniel greeted George with his normal warm notions. "Looking fine this morning, Mr. George."

"As you, Mr. Hise."

The men chuckled at their ritual and quickly went to work on the day's tasks.

Daniel began, "I will need you to paint the doubletrees I made for David Woodruff first thing. They will need a bit of time to dry, and I believe a second coat will be required."

"I will start them at once."

George knew his way around Daniel's blacksmith shop. His consistent work schedule made him a valuable asset to Daniel. The first coat of paint was completed just as the sun rose. The men stood in the open doorway sipping a hot cup of coffee.

"How is your freedom money holding up, George?"

"Progress has been slow, sir. I have six dollars set aside and a few odd cents. I had to use up a bit to buy my mare." He looked over at his pitiful blind horse, "By the looks of her I may be usin' up a bit more. She's gone blind on me. Can't see much but shadows anymore." He started to chuckle, "But she sure knows her way here. She likes Tuesday. It seems she prances just a bit higher when she knows I am close."

Daniel eyed George curiously as he spoke. He was not certain if George was speaking of his mare or himself. He looked toward the kitchen where Mim once stood. His eyes returned to George's horse.

"She has a few years left, I trust. She has a strong back and a stout will to serve. You can lead her when she cannot see the way." Daniel stroked her mane. "She adores you. You do not need strong eyes to see that!" Daniel finished his last sip of coffee, "Six dollars? Well, we best get back to work so you can add a bit to that today."

They heard the hooves of a single galloping horse approaching. The rider jumped the stone wall at the end of the drive and headed straight for the barn. He pulled the reins; the horse reared.

His voice sliced through the thin morning air, "Slave Holders are here. They are coming for George!" He turned his horse and disappeared into the open field.

George ran to the trap door in the floor of the bank barn that led to the underground tunnel. His thick fingers slid the bolt closed to block their entrance. In the darkness he managed to find the matches and candle stubs and crawled five feet into the tunnel before striking.

The burst of light lit the walls. Instinct forced his body against the red brick. He heard the sound of the approaching horsemen. He slid on his stomach until his fingers reached the edge of the tunnel. He snuffed out the candle flame and moved into the safety of the stonewalled room.

The Slave Holders burst through Daniel's barn door. The leader's tone was sharp and vaulted. "We came for the slave named George that you are harboring here."

Daniel wiped the fresh paint from his hands with a dry rag. "Gentlemen, you have arrived just in time to assist me in the lifting of the doubletrees."

"We came for the runaway slave!"

Daniel smirked, "Where did you hear such things?"

The man slid from his saddle and moved close to Daniel. His words came through his discolored teeth, "We were sent to find and return this slave to his Master and owner, Samuel Ward of Oak Bend Georgia. Do you hinder our search?"

Daniel whistled. Margaret appeared through the back door. "Margaret, these men are here to find a slave named…." He looked at one of the men to finish.

"George."

"A slave named George. Show them in."

Whether or not a marshal accompanied the Slave Holders, it was forbidden by law to deny their access. Margaret moved from the doorway.

George listened from the room below their feet. He held his breath. With his body again pressed against the wall, he counted five men.

Every door was opened, closed, and reopened. Each bed was upturned. The curtains were pulled from their rods and thrown on the floor. In the southwest bedroom one of the men emptied the closet onto the inverted bed. He tapped on the side closet wall.

"I have found something!" echoed through the house.

Another man joined him as he gently tapped again on the wall. "It's hollow."

A second man joined them and pushed him aside. The weight of his body fell against the flimsy board, and it collapsed without hindrance. He landed in the adjacent closet covered in dresses and petticoats. The room burst into laughter. The fabric covered his flushed face.

When the leader entered the room, a command of silence froze the men's voices. He was not amused.

"I find nothing here. The cobbler took our one-hundred dollars and sent us on a wild chase." He pulled the lingerie from his rider's face. "I think we need to pay him another visit." His eyes echoed his anger.

Daniel was loading the first of his doubletrees onto the wagon when the group stormed out of the house. They jumped onto their horses and rode toward town.

"Gentlemen, what of my doubletrees?" he called after them. The gaiety of his laughter tumbled to gravity when he heard George open the latch on the trap door.

"To the wagon, George!"

George slid into the place he dubbed as his third home — the narrow space of the false-bottom buckboard. Daniel loaded the single-coated doubletrees over the hidden opening. He brought both fingers to his lips and whistled to signal his wife. She waved in acknowledgement from the kitchen.

"Yet love will dream, and faith will trust, that somewhere, somehow, meet we must." Daniel's words gently tossed to his wife were met with a smile.

Within two minutes the wagon headed toward the country. Daniel's heart raced until Unserheim had slipped from view. He moved his wagon through a series of unmarked paths and less traveled roads until he arrived at Jonas Cattell's property northwest of town.

With Daniel's whistle, Jonas moved into action. The buckboard shuddered as they raced down the well-traveled path. Trees on either side strategically planted within inches of one another created a natural screen from the peering eyes of the Copperheads and their spies. The wagon jolted to a stop at a lower level door.

George slid open the hidden latch and sprang from his captivity as if it was a written script. The men moved the doubletrees back into place while George ran into the house. He took the stairs three at a time reaching the top within seconds. Without stopping he forced his body through the opening in the back of a fireplace that Jonas had made ready by removing the fireback.

Once inside the small hidden room behind the fireplace, George slid the cast iron fireback into place. He heard the roar of a fire from the other side of the metal door that was built to further conceal his whereabouts.

He settled his body into a corner and drank the glass of water that had been placed for his comfort. Beside the glass sat a bowl of stew and two thick slices of bread. George soaked the bread in the gravy and enjoyed each bite until it was gone. He closed his eyes to rest for a long stay in the country. He would remain in the Cattell home until the Slave Holders stopped looking for him. He had been there before, and he would surely return.

He allowed his thoughts to drift to the day he would stand before Master Ward with fifty dollars in his hand to buy his freedom. A broad smile covered his face. He drifted to sleep clinging to pleasant dreams.

29

Rebecca lay awake in her bed. It was a Thursday in late October. Abigail had been gone for over two years. Nathaniel, with George's help, had aided many slaves toward freedom as they had done this night. She tried to recall the names, but many simply referred to themselves by their slave number. She thought it odd that a group of people so desperate to taste freedom permitted themselves to be reduced to that degradation.

Salem's closest slave auction house was in Wheeling, Virginia. Many abolitionists attended those sales to purchase the slaves. Once safely outside of the city, the slaves were told they were free. Nathaniel had attended only twice but aided in the funding as much as he was able.

Before the "property" was sold, a gross inspection took place. This demeaning process rarely took place behind closed doors and was often performed in the company of the interested buyers. Not a sound was permitted during the inspection, even if the probes resulted in the development of blood. More often than not, the slaves appeared before the crowd stripped of everything, including their pride.

Most of the able-bodied males sold for seven to eight hundred dollars. If a man was labeled as a "prime cotton picker," he could bring upwards of one thousand. Most male babies that were marked as "good bones" sold for four-hundred dollars. The woman and female children sold for significantly less even though their abilities in the field, kitchen, or the bedroom were considered invaluable.

All slave families were purposely split apart. The only exception was if the plantation's wet nurse could not nourish a newborn. Only then was the baby allowed to stay with its birth mother.

Once the property was purchased, they were shackled together until they could be labeled. Many of the slaves were burned with a cattle branding iron as well as fitted with a slave tag. Although Samuel insisted his goods be given a Christian name, most masters referred to their slaves as simple numbers.

The sight of a whip stifled the cries of separation and pain quickly. Most slaves could expect at least one "moderate whipping" in their lifetime. This beating was counted as thirty lashes. Rebecca shuddered at the thought of how many moderate whippings George had endured. She knew without the intervention of Lilly and Lacey that George would not have lived to taste freedom.

On this evening a young slave named Ramon sought safety in their home. He had long been separated from his father, also so named, and mother, Linney.

Ramon, in one of those rare situations, was able to stay with his mother as a newborn. Because the plantation did not have a viable replacement, Linney was granted the privilege to raise her son, at least for a few years.

When Ramon reached the age of eight, he was sold to a neighboring plantation in Georgia. Three times he escaped and made the short trip back to his mother. His last escape was kept secret for nearly one month until the master's son saw Ramon hiding amidst the Camellias. He was pulled from the bushes, beaten, and returned.

Ramon never revisited his mother. Instead he set his sights on finding his father. It wasn't until his last effort to escape that Ramon heard of the fate of his father; his body was located on Otter Island next to a man named Tobias.

Ramon traveled the same route to liberty as many before him, including George. When the door of the railcar flew open at the train's Salem stop, George greeted the escaped slave. He jumped on the back of the saddle with George and fled from the tracks while the others stayed behind to conceal their covert operation.

Nathaniel rode hard tonight. His heart was uneasy, and George's mare struggled to keep the pace with the extra rider. When the men reached the house, they hurried to the raised-paneled hallway. George and Ramon hid in the small room together while Nathaniel cared for their horses.

After a few moments of silence, Ramon whispered, "Your name George?"

"Yes," his reply was hesitant.

Ramon reached inside his pocket and pulled out a crumpled envelope. Embarrassed at its condition, he placed it on the floor and smoothed it out at best as he could. His hand shook as he extended it to George.

"Go on, takes it. It's for you."

The room was too dark to read the letter, but George was able to see Lilly's penmanship. "Where did you find this?"

152

"No suh, I didn't find it, a lady gives it to me. Pretty lady she was. She says you gives this to George. He will be in Salem wif you. You find him and gives this to him. It is very important." He smiled at his story and added, "I gots reward money to gives it to you. Be a nice start for my freedom. Yep, a nice start." Ramon smiled and nodded his head at the thought of living free.

George's heart raced. He wondered what the letter held. He would have to wait.

"It's too dark to reads it in here. Yes, suh, too dark." He peered at George, "Can you read?"

George fanned the letter in the air, "Yes, sir. She taught me."

Within moments, Ramon's quiet snores filled the room, yet sleep eluded George. After repeatedly opening the letter in the darkness and holding it inches from his face, George finally gave up. He fell asleep clutching the letter to his chest listening to Ramon's rhythmic breath.

The sound of the opening lock woke the men. Nathaniel spoke in haste, "The time has come." He motioned for Ramon to follow and turned to address George, "You must stay. We fear of watchful eyes."

George slipped through the passageway and crept to the windowed room. He watched Nathaniel drive the seemingly empty buckboard down the path toward Salem. He turned at the shuffle of feet from behind him. Rebecca smiled at him.

George reached into his pocket and withdrew the letter. His hand trembled while he traced Lilly's inscription.

"Ramon gave this to me last night." His words splintered. "I…it was dark. I have not read it."

"Then, read it to me," Rebecca begged.

"I am filled with," he stopped. Thoughts of fear mingled with joy, and he was unable to finish.

"Good news or bad, you must read it to know."

George nodded, opened the letter, and read its contents.

My dearest George,

Only yesterday Father went to be with the Lord. I fear he suffered greatly for his sins. However it was with his dying breath that the words of freedom rang out for you, George. Enclosed within this package are the appropriate papers for your liberty. Father died clutching the exact payment necessary for this to be possible. You, George, are free from slavery.

I have heard word of your good health and whereabouts through many of the same sources we have shared. This letter traveled the same path that led you to independence.

Please search your heart to forgive Father, for his measures ultimately calmed his spirit. I am afraid his previous actions were his undoing.

Be well, be happy, and be free.

Always,
Lilly

Rebecca's face flooded with tears. She wrapped her arms around George and squealed while he lifted her body in the air and swung her in a tight circle. They laughed, cried, and returned again to laughter. Their bodies slipped to the floor, dizzy from the twirl as well as the news.

George read the letter to her three times before his eyes finally settled on the last line. He repeated it with pride, "Be well, be happy, and be free."

With Lilly's letter and documentation clasped in his hand an impromptu groan rose from deep within. With it came the release of bondage, years of toil and strife pulled from him without thought or care. The natural release came as no surprise to him. For the first time in his life, George felt peace.

"Miss Rebecca, I am a free man." He lifted his hands and voice. "*Free*...free!" George stood up, planted his feet, and waved his hand in the air. His voice reflected his mood as he proclaimed, "I, George, am free from slavery!"

30

*N*athaniel slipped through the back door undetected. The sound of celebration filled the house. He rushed up the flight of stairs to the top and found George fanning his news to all who would listen. Within minutes, Nathaniel joined in the gaiety. They danced in a circle, shouted proclamations, cried, laughed, and danced some more, all with booming voices that ratted the windows.

Nathaniel pushed the sobering thought of his news from his lips. He dreaded the idea of spoiling this joyous moment, yet his eyes could not shade his concern and he watched George's smile slide from his face.

Nathaniel tried to recover the mood. "This is serious news! George, you are a free man!"

George knew his friend well. He saw the flash of concern revealed from deep within. He moved closer to Nathaniel. "What is it, Nathaniel?"

Again, he tried to avoid the subject. Subconsciously his hand covered the letter in his pocket. "It can wait, George."

156

"Your eyes speak differently."

Nathaniel shook his head. "I do not want to spoil this moment, though I am certain you need to know." He pulled the parchment from his coat and eyed George as he read its contents. "It came to me through Ramon." Nathaniel lowered his voice. "It seems he carried much news."

George read the words silently. Word of Monroe's capture cast a dark shadow across his face. He cursed the currier for bringing this news to them. In frustration, he pounded his fist on the table toppling the vase of spent flowers. Water puddled around his clenched hand.

Nathaniel eyed him curiously. "The letter makes no mention of Mim?"

George shook his bowed head. "I shudder to think what may follow. The atrocities that befall those captured are not easily forgotten. Monroe has lost one hand by his master's rage. I fear…."

"You fear Otter Island?"

George nodded, "Yes. I fear the worst." Tears flooded his eyes, "And what of Mim?"

Nathaniel took the tattered letter from his friend and scanned the words. "There is no mention of another traveler. It seems he was alone."

"Then what has become of Mim? When they left together on the fourth night of their stay at Unserheim, they bound allegiance to each other." His words were frantic.

"George, we must not assume the worst. We will try to find word, if not by our own doing, by Mim's. She will contact you."

"My mind fears the worst, yet my heart speaks differently."

"Then listen to your heart. It will guide you best."

157

George's mind trailed from Nathaniel's words of comfort. He allowed his heart to take him back to his first few days in Salem, to his moments with Mim. A usual slave stay at Unserheim was only until nightfall when they were moved on to the next freedom house by cover of the dark, but with the Copperheads' close watch Nathaniel thought it best for George, Mim, and Monroe to remain hidden until they lost interest. The slaves remained together for three nights.

As George recalled on his second evening at Unserheim, Monroe arrived on foot. Two men accompanied him. When they knocked on the south side door, Monroe was ushered into the windowless receiving room. Daniel showed him to the winter bedroom where George and Mim were sleeping.

He remembered how Mim jumped from her bed and embraced her brother. She insisted he rest in her bed. George did not object to sharing his with her.

She lay beside him in the dark. The smell of her freshly washed hair was intoxicating. He closed off his thoughts and listened to Monroe talk for nearly an hour about his ride and near capture. Mim covered her mouth in horror as he spoke.

Even in those early moments George could not remove his eyes from her. Monroe's tale was adventurous, filled with angst and desire, but it did not hold George's interest. He reminded his ears to focus on Monroe's story while his eyes studied Mim.

"They was waitin' at the en' of the train," Monroe whispered. "Three men jump us when wesa rode pas'em. Our horse raise up in the air and done kicked the rider off his. The other two stayed back. Mus'a been 'fraid cuz they stayed back." He lowered his voice, "Isa stayed jus one night in the country they calls it. Then wesa wait for the ness night and crept our way here. The man says Isa be safe here. And then says usa bof here too." A wide grin came across his face, "Isa sure nuf glad to see you bof."

Long after he finished his story, George remembered lying awake. Never in his life had he shared a bed with a woman. Her body rose and fell with each soft breath. George fell asleep dreaming his arms were wrapped around her.

Sunlight streamed in the east window. It was high in the morning sky. George listened for sounds of movement in the house, but all was quiet.

He remembered sliding from underneath the covers. Mim stirred but continued to sleep. Monroe snored softly from under his pillow. His body rested on top of the blankets. Only his head was covered. George smiled and slipped from the room. When he entered the barn, he interrupted a conversation between Daniel and Nathaniel.

"I am not certain that is the best course," Nathaniel spoke with reservation. "I think Canada by way of the safe houses is best. You know what happens when they travel in numbers."

"We are easier to capture." The men were startled by George's presence.

Nathaniel nodded in agreement and echoed, "Yes, you are right, George. You are an easier target. Many of the safe houses cannot harbor three slaves. Most can only hold two and fewer, only one."

"We were discussing the best way to ensure all of your safety," Daniel added.

George stared at the two men. Their faces were grave. "If it is best, I will stay."

"But George...."

"Let Monroe and his sister go together," he interrupted. "I have come this far alone. I can continue alone."

"So be it," Nathaniel agreed. "But before you continue on your own, you will stay with me. Suspicions are heavy on Daniel. After their departure we will travel south to my home at midnight."

George's heart sank at the words. He knew it was safer for them to separate, but he had grown fond of Mim and was saddened at the thought of not spending another night in her company. He walked back to the house to share the news.

Monroe spent the afternoon in the company of Nathaniel and Daniel. Rebecca and Margaret prepared the noon and evening meals while Mim and George enjoyed the day in quiet conversation.

Mim listened intently as George spoke of Oak Bend, Master Ward and his daughters. He explained how Lacey with Lilly's help secreted a plan for his escape. He shared his dreams and desires, all but for her. Mim's face was lit with admiration as he spoke. When he finished speaking, he urged Mim to share her history. She spoke through tears, for her own story was painful to recall.

When her mother was purchased at auction house in South Carolina, her master favored his new slave and decided to keep her separate from the rest. He prepared a special bedroom in the main house, one in which only he held the key. He lay with her that first evening and remained for three nights. Nine months later she gave birth to a daughter.

Over the next fifteen years, she had ten pregnancies, but only reared four children — three boys and Mim. She was a valued wet nurse by day and a desire for the master at night. Felma had accepted her fate as his personal pet until the birth of her third son.

Monroe was a troublesome child. He cried constantly with colic and refused his mother's milk. His master became increasing agitated with the amount of attention given to this annoying child, for it took away Felma's attention and his pleasure.

As Monroe grew, his color began to deepen. The master became convinced that this child was not his own. Although Felma had never been with another, she could not persuade him. Monroe was taken from her at age six and sold at the auction.

The relationship between Felma and her master quickly curdled. Often, she refused his advances. He began to beat her for the denial. She died in the sweatbox pregnant for the tenth time.

In the years following Felma's death, the lady of the manor began to fear for Mim and sent her away to finishing school. Her obvious difference in appearance made her a target for the white girls, but the instructress acted as a buffer. After a few months, the mockery ceased.

She became skilled in stitching and speech. She grew into a beautiful, charming woman, and her classmates became jealous. The instructress convinced the Lady to allow her return to the plantation, but she feared Mim would capture the master's attention or worse — teach the slaves to read and write — so the Lady secretly sent her to live with her brother.

It was a bittersweet reunion. Monroe, now twenty, had already suffered the loss of his hand when Mim arrived, and the rest of his band criticized her proper ways. Her light skin, hair, and eyes made her an obvious target, and it wasn't long before her new master noticed her. Monroe decided to flee before she was corrupted.

They spent the first few months in the swamp with others who had escaped and made their homes on the muddy water with the alligators and snakes. She explained how these people lived, their diet, and hunting techniques. She explained how she lost her shoe in the thick muck, and it was the first time George heard her laugh. It was in the sweetness of her laughter that he fell in love.

They sat together through their last meal at Unserheim. Nerves stole George's appetite. He played with his food until the touch of Mim's hand urged him to eat.

"You must keep up your strength," she whispered, "...for me, for us."

When dinner had ended, they excused themselves for more whispered talk. When the evening sky grew dark, their mouths became silent. Tears and smiles flooded their faces.

At midnight Monroe entered the dark, silent room. "'Tis time."

Mim leapt into George's arms and sobbed. They whispered quietly together. The moisture of her tender kiss lingered on George's lips. They did not speak when she exited the room.

George recalled standing on the front porch and watching their shadows slide from sight. He had left many things unsaid and wished for the opportunity to relive their last few moments together. Looking back, he feared that the chance to speak his thoughts were lost as it had been nearly one year since he last saw Mim.

His hand trembled as his thoughts returned to the present. His eyes struggled to focus on the penned words that he held in his hand.

Nathaniel watched his friend stare at the crumpled piece of paper. He took the letter from George and read it again.

George,

I plead for your help. I have been captured in Michigan and am bound for the Carolinas. I was a fool to not continue to Canada. I was lured into the safety of our numbers and decided to stay with the others. I could not have been more wrong. Please help if you can. I fear the worst in my return.

Monroe&

George's face was twisted as he peered over his friend's shoulder. "What puzzles me is these are not his words."

"But it carries his name," Nathaniel protested.

"His signature I see, but this speech is not his. The words sound more of Mim."

With the mention of her name, his eyes fell on Monroe's signature. A scrolled symbol appeared after the letter e. It was a sign. He was not alone.

"Nathaniel!" Desperation covered his face. He pointed to the ampersand. "They are together. Mim has been taken!"

31

Rebecca's wagon bounced over the dirt roads that led into town. Her errands were followed in a systematic pattern, although today she did not have time for the confectionary. She drew a deep breath of its sweetness as she passed the double doors.

Her skeptic eyes searched the crowd for strange faces. Today, Salem seemed to be filled with sordid characters. A small group of men led by one woman moved from shop to shop. They entered and exited without purchasing. It seemed they were intent on gathering information.

One man in particular seemed slightly familiar to Rebecca. Twice their eyes met, and she quickly looked away. He had a strange gait. She tried to place their meeting but could not.

Most of the townsmen were uneasy with their questions. They flashed abolitionists' coins and swore secrecy and loyalty, but when they spent a bit longer in the cobbler's shop, their lie was revealed.

Rebecca was careful to avoid them. She spoke to no one as she walked briskly toward her passing of Daniel. His face was grave, yet the motion of placing a bit of parchment in her palm became so fluid it was done without feeling. Rebecca buried the paper in her handkerchief and tucked it deep within her corset. She left town with a wagon loaded with supplies and a light heart for another slave coming to be free.

She reached the woods' edge before the failing light. The red and orange hues of the setting sun whispered through a few openings of the dense growth. She rode her wagon to the center of the clearing and waited for the men to appear. No one came.

She grew anxious. She retraced the day's events to be sure she had not missed an important detail that would have made her deviate from the usual plan. Convinced she had not overlooked any signs, she jumped from the wagon seat and peered behind the perimeter trunks. Only silence greeted her.

She pulled her handkerchief from her corset. The note floated to the ground. She stared at the numbers – 2 – 17—3.

Specific instructions were given when these freedom rides began. Each player had his or her exact role. Rebecca's was the message giver. She was told to wait until the men who would be riding received the information. As the day's final light slid from the sky, she was filled with dread. Something was terribly wrong.

She paced in the clearing. Twilight turned to dusk, and then dusk to dark. She waited for nearly two hours.

Her horse became anxious. He pawed at the ground and tossed his head. His snorts were short and forceful. Rebecca knew he sensed danger. She jumped onto the wagon and covered herself.

As the darkness surrounded her, each noise was magnified. Her body jumped at the sound of a cracking stick or the rustling of the leaves. A pair of raccoons chattered from a nearby tree. She never moved.

Many times she entertained the thought of abandoning the mission. She knew the lives of these two slaves depended on her method of delivery. If she failed to get the information to the abolitionists, the slaves would not be rescued and would be discovered at the next train stop. They would be beaten and either returned to their masters for bounty or killed. A shiver moved through her body. The grave importance of her part in this freedom call had never been so intense.

She tried to occupy her mind with other thoughts, but the woods seemed to come alive with sounds. She slid the blanket from her head. Ten men stood around her wagon. She jumped at surprise.

"I have been waiting and worried with fear of your absence," she chastised.

"We were much delayed in our arrival. We were pursued by others." He lowered his head, "Three were captured."

Rebecca gasped at the words, "What has become of them?"

"We know not."

"What were their names?"

The man stammered at the question. Another stepped forward in the darkness to answer, "Do not be concerned with the names, Rebecca. They are not of yours. Nathaniel is safe. Though we must quickly gather your information and be off. Your journey home must be direct and swift, for I also fear for your safety."

Rebecca watched his actions as he spoke. She did not recognize his face. Something in his mannerisms seemed strangely familiar. She shivered at his calling of her name and that of her father's. That was never done.

She stiffened her back and commanded, "Be revealed to me!" She climbed over the wagon seat and sat down.

The men obeyed. One by one they stepped into her view. Darkness covered their faces. Rebecca reached for the reins. Their bodies were covered with black cloaks. In one hand each man's hand held an abolitionist's coin; in the other, an iron rod.

Large beech trees lined the perimeter of the clearing. A fallen matriarch created the void for the center. The forest floor was barren under their massive trunks, but beyond the reach of their roots the undergrowth flourished. Whispered motion came from beyond the thick covering.

The labyrinth of the beech's limbs blanketed any light from the moon. Rebecca struggled to examine their faces in the dappled soft light. She knew not one man's face.

Thoughts of her mother stole her attention. Visions of her bludgeoned body paralyzed her. The men spoke in hushed whispers, but her mind could not hear. She had no memory of snapping the reins. Her horse leapt into action.

The men quickly closed the opening with their bodies. Their arms flung wildly calling for her to halt.

The wagon jostled over the tree roots and nearly overturned. Rebecca's eyes were focused on escape. She never saw the two men who were trampled by her horse, yet their screams filled her ears.

They ran in a flurry. Her cargo spilled from the buckboard with each rock or root. They burst through the edge of the woods. The wagon rattled from the speed. The horse ran feverishly. His feet no longer held the path. They were running blind.

Her wheels wobbled from their speed. Two riders appeared by her side. She snapped the reins again.

Without warning, the left side of the wagon leapt into the air. The horse whinnied in fear. The back weight shifted and overturned them. The crash broke the tongue and the horse continued to run.

Rebecca was thrown into the air. Her movement seemed slow; yet she knew it was only an instant. She landed onto the hardened ground. Her body was contorted and unable to move. Her head spun and swooned from the blow.

The men slid from their horses and ran to her side. Afraid to move her body, they called to her.

"The note, Rebecca!"

His face was close to hers. It was then she recognized him from town earlier that day. He walked with a limp. Her vision narrowed and faded to black.

*N*athaniel sat at the table wringing his hands. Rebecca's absence unnerved him.

"Why did I agree to her involvement? She is but a girl," his head swayed in disbelief.

George sat beside him at the dining room table. He too was filled with concern.

He patted the back of Nathaniel's hand.

"She will return soon, sir."

"Abigail warned me; nonetheless, her advice I did not heed."

George looked through the window. "It is not yet dark. She will come." His words were spoken with confidence, yet his heart spoke a different tale, one he could not speak.

They sat in silence for nearly an hour. The windows grew black with night. Nathaniel rose from the table.

"It has been too long. I must go."

"No sir, I will go. You stay here to greet her return. I will go to the clearing. If I do not find her there, I will take the path to town." He placed his hand on Nathaniel's shoulder. "I will return with her if not she first."

"No, George. I can no longer sit idly by. I must find my little girl."

169

"We will both go. I will travel by way of the clearing."

"And I will search beyond."

Their paths carried them together until the edge of the woods. George entered through the thicket while Nathaniel rode the perimeter and followed the path toward Salem.

Rebecca burst through the door dragging the hem of her soiled and tattered dress. Her body was bloody and stiff.

"Father! George!" her shouts filled the house.

She ran up the back staircase and slid through the paneled hallway. She opened the wood door to the hidden room and whispered. No reply came. She called for her father throughout the house. It was silent.

Two cups of unfinished coffee sat on the dining room table. The chairs were drawn away from a hasty retreat. She wrapped her hands around one of the cups. It was cold.

She forced her tired body to climb the stairs to her bedroom. She filled her washbowl with the cool water from her pitcher and began to bathe. The liquid quickly turned to deep red. She changed the water until her pitcher was empty.

Weary from the trauma she collapsed on her bed. Guilt consumed her. She had failed her father and the men who would be traveling on the train tomorrow evening. She forced thoughts of their capture and return from her mind. Reflection of her betrayal and incompetence moved her to tears. She did not hear her father's return.

33

*N*athaniel returned home from his fourth freedom call in one week. It was only Wednesday. The October leaves had just begun to share their splendor of colors, but he was too preoccupied to notice.

It had been two years almost to the day since Rebecca's last involvement. Many times since that evening she tried to explain to her father, but he seemed distant and uncaring. Nathaniel refused to discuss her reinstatement.

She traveled into town once a week as normal to gather supplies. On each visit she passed Daniel, but no parchment was placed in her palm. At times, she pulled her handkerchief from her corset and read the last set of numbers that were entrusted to her. She cried through the guilt, the loss of purpose, but mostly she cried for the strained relationship it caused with her father.

Nathaniel's freedom calls took him away most evenings and into the early morning hours. George worked on the farm taking care of animals and fields while Nathaniel spent the days riding with rods. On occasion, George rode with Nathaniel, but their rides together became less frequent.

Dimness cast a shadow across George's face since the news of Monroe and Mim's capture. After two years the hope of her safety dwindled a bit each day. He kept a candle lit in the second upstairs window of Nathaniel's freedom house. As he struck the match, he whispered a prayer for Mim's return.

Rebecca found herself alone most of the time. She took long strolls in the fields, swam in the calm pool of their stream, and picked bouquets of wildflowers. Sometimes she would place them in a vase on the dining room table, but most of the time she took them to Hope Cemetery.

It was in Hope that her mother was buried. Rebecca placed the flowers on her mother's grave. She tended to an unearthed patch of dirt just beyond Abigail's headstone. It was a troublesome bit, one that never held grass. Rebecca did all she could to encourage growth, but the ground seemed to promote turmoil.

Most of the times, Rebecca stared at the memorial. The etched words

Abigail Wentworth Kristol
May 1860

evoked many tearful afternoons. She thought it odd that her mother's memory was reduced to a month. Nathaniel was so heartbroken with her murder that he could not bring himself to speak of the day. Recalling the month was difficult enough.

At the Kristol homestead, Rebecca longed for conversations with her father. Often, they sat in silence. She tried to speak of light affairs to her father, but he would not respond. She apologized for her failure each time they sat together. Nathaniel rarely retorted. If any words left his lips, they were, "It was my fault." Those days, he hung his head and cried.

Once, Rebecca overheard a conversation between her father and George. She had just finished arranging her vase of wildflowers.

"Nathaniel, must you ride again tonight?"

"It is my duty, George. My calling."

"But others may be called. You need rest."

"Rest?" he shouted. "What if I had spoken such things the night you arrived, George?"

George had been accustomed to Nathaniel's agitated state. "Sir, I mean no disrespect. Your eyes are sickly with pain."

"Yes, I am tired, but I must go."

"Why do you punish yourself? How could you have known?"

"She was a child! A child! What kind of father involves a baby to do man's work?"

"Her intelligence was shown in her years. She could not have known." His voice became softer, "Please, Nathaniel, do not punish yourself for what could not have been helped. It is a grave business. One both of you willingly accepted."

"But so young."

"And wise. She carried out your wishes not for your approval, but for the honor of doing what is right. She followed her heart. Not many men are brave enough to boast of that." He placed his hand on Nathaniel's shoulders. "She has tried many times to apologize, yet your eyes are blind."

George walked through the wide doorframe into the kitchen. He wrapped his hands around Rebecca's flowers and carried them to the dining room table. An empty doily waited for the honor of placement.

"These are from her. As a token of apology." He extended the bouquet to Nathaniel. "Please take these in acceptance."

Nathaniel hugged the vase and wept. Rebecca smiled from the doorway as her father placed the arrangement in the center of the table. That day marked the time of hushed sorrows and apologies to end. Healing could now begin. Rebecca's words were heard, spoken loudly through a gift of flowers.

34

The next few weeks the Kristol house was filled with activities. Several farm hands were hired to help tend the harvest. The remaining bales of the alfalfa/timothy mix of second crop were moved to make room for the third cutting. The horse and cow stalls were cleared and layered with fresh straw. The corncribs were filled, and the prize hog was butchered and hung for salt curing.

Nathaniel hired a group of women for their knowledge in the kitchen. One of the ladies was Adah Carter. She had lived in the area as a freed slave since 1827 thanks to an abolitionist named Samuel Palmer who paid four hundred dollars for her freedom. Adah felt indebted to the people of the movement and due to the recent troubles that befell the Kristol family she felt obligated to offer help. She was a kind woman in her early sixties who had great knowledge of preserving food. Her consistent hum as she moved about the kitchen lured the others to follow. Many nimble hands made light of the work.

Not only did the women prepare the meals for all involved but also cleaned, washed, and primed the vegetables for canning. Fennel, thyme, dill, rosemary, and borage flowers were harvested from the herb garden. Their savory scents and flavors would bring fullness to the processed goods.

A large kettle hung in the yard over a strong fire that had been stoked and fed for several days. The women preserved beets, apples, pickles, squash, and beans. They processed fresh pork as well as a few chickens that had stopped laying eggs. They dug potatoes, turnips, and carrots and placed them in layers of straw in the fruit cellar. Finally, they shucked black walnuts and filled three oversized baskets to dry in the barn's loft over the winter months.

When most of the autumn's harvest was complete, they prepared a feast for all involved in the hard weeks of labor. A turkey with a wide variety of the fresh vegetables was served. When everyone was fully satisfied, the women placed the rest of the stew in mason jars and boiled them in a water bath. Once cooled, they were placed on a shelf in the cold cellar with the rest of the month's work.

Rebecca did not take part in the fun. Her normal gaiety turned sour with the arrival of the women. Their bustling around her kitchen made her feel inept and it was easier to move out of their way. She enjoyed quiet moments, not a flurry of activity.

She watched from her bedroom window as one of the women carried out the house rugs. She hung them on the line and began to beat the dust from them. The consistent sound of the wire rugbeater's throng made her long for her mother.

She ran from the house away from the sound. Her feet carried her through a field where she normally picked lavish wildflower bouquets, but today most of the flowers were spent. She managed to find a few sprigs of purple fall asters, mint leaves, and one lone euphorbia. She sighed at the pitiful sight of her bouquet.

Before she realized, she had walked the entire way to the cemetery. Much of the walk she could not recall. She collapsed at her mother's grave. The flowers had withered in her hand.

"I just could not stay, Mother. I fear I am overwhelmed. This is where I choose to be." She glanced at her flowers. "It is all I could find. Winter is coming. Even the flowers whisper of its signs." She glanced up at the evening sky. "There is an unsettled coolness in the breeze. Trouble is brewing."

Most of her time spent in the cemetery was in solitude. This evening she noticed many visitors. Meager field flowers were presented to their loved ones. Overcome with curiosity Rebecca moved closer to them.

One particular spot caught her attention. It was on one of the highest knolls in the cemetery. No gravestones had yet been set; only a small sapling grew there. Its trunk split into two equal parts just a few inches above the ground. In the crux a large bouquet of roses was placed. Rebecca fingered their petals. Fragrance filled the air.

She looked again at the peculiar split in the trunk. "Visions of what is to come," she whispered and walked back to her mother. She lay her head in the arms of an oak tree and fell fast sleep.

When she woke the following morning, she was surprised no stiffness lingered from sleeping on the hard earth. Voices filled her ears. The cemetery was teeming with people for a funeral. She pulled her knees to her chest and watched. Most slipped past without a glance in her direction, only a few noticed her. They looked at Rebecca with wide eyes but never spoke a word. Within an hour she was alone.

Almost on cue, the wind kicked dust in Rebecca's face and when she had cleared her eyes, she saw a young woman standing by the special tree. Her face was buried in the bouquet of roses. She replaced her gift with a gathering of wildflowers.

A young man moved from the nearby shadows. He smiled at Rebecca's curiosity from a distance, and then turned to greet his female suitor. They embraced and walked together in the empty cemetery. Their bodies moved in harmony until they disappeared from view.

Rebecca ran to the top of the knoll. When she caught sight, only the woman remained. She walked past Rebecca without a sound or recognition.

In the next few weeks, Rebecca noticed this couple nearly every day. The ritual seemed to repeat the same pattern. The gentleman always placed a bouquet of roses. Where he gathered such beauty was a mystery to Rebecca, for the roses of her mother's garden had long developed into ripening rose hips. The young woman gathered her spray from the fields.

Rebecca longed for a love to be manifested in his way — for a young man to bring his affection and longing through the voice of flowers and wait for his lady to return the gesture. She permitted her mind to wander into a place of rest and love. She wondered if she would ever feel the beauty.

GEORGE

George grew more troubled over Nathaniel's failing health with each passing day. He had long given up pleading for his friend to rest and let the others ride to ease his burden. Nathaniel was driven. His voice for freedom became louder, more pronounced. He mirrored Daniel's commitment and dedication, uncaring of what may become of him.

The Copperheads, especially Hanna Prenstrum's group, watched his home south of Salem heavily. Hanna grew more anxious to infiltrate the abolitionists and destroy those involved. In the past four years, only once had her riders disguised as one of the freedom fighters spoiled a freedom call. Her heart grew hard as she narrowed her sights on one man — Nathaniel.

Hanna carried the Dietz lantern to the center beam and struck a match. The light sparked a sense of cheerfulness that was quickly dampened by her mood. The flame settled to a soft glow. Even it seemed to obey her desires.

She walked the length of her barn floor for the third time. Each step quickened and echoed louder until the building was filled with her agitation. Twice she peered out into the darkness. She was alone.

"Where is he?" she spat on the ground.

Subconsciously her hands twisted the paper she held. It was a note from her sister in Georgia pleading for help. She stared at the letter warped like ribbon candy dampened from sweat.

The night's voices were silenced by the approaching sound of a single horse. It ran with urgency. Hanna crossed her arms and tapped her foot. The rider walked into the dimly lit barn leading his horse.

"You are late!" she scoffed.

"It could not be helped." He hung his head as Hanna huffed at his response.

The young man before her was one of her Moles. He was tall, gangly, and appeared to be in his early twenties. His eyes were dark and shadowed by the brim of his hat. He seldom made eye contact and spoke in an even hushed tone. His demeanor seemed humble until he held an iron rod in his hands. Then, his true personality was revealed.

His name was Trey Cabot. He lived on the adjacent farm and was summoned by Hanna all hours of the night. He rarely disappointed her. He was edgy, stiff, and cunning.

"Gather the men tomorrow," she spoke in whispers. "Bring them all to me at midnight."

"For a mission?" his voice was tight.

"For an understanding," she scoffed. "There can be no mission until we are united for one cause. All too often important information has slipped through our hands. The freedom fighters are privy to our every move." She eyed him suspiciously. "Ask yourself why."

He swallowed hard at her peering eyes. "But what can be done? They are many and we are few."

"That is a poor excuse!" Anger contorted her face. "They may have numbers, but we have might. I tire of their paraded success."

"They scream it."

"And we must be louder. Our plan needs revision. Bring me all of the men. I will reveal our new order, and we must rid ourselves of the chaff." She pounded her foot to punctuate her point.

"Chaff?" he asked timidly.

She leaned into him and lowered her voice, "A conspirator runs with us. He must be eliminated."

He swallowed hard for the second time. Hanna was a force not to be taken lightly. He knew she meant business, and the night would reveal a few surprises.

Her order scattered his thoughts. "Now go. Gather the men. Tomorrow at midnight we shall become what we were meant to be." She walked out of the barn but stopped at the door. She called from over her shoulder, "And tell the men to dress for a ride!" She disappeared through a cloud of dust thrown from her boots.

Silently, another slipped from the haymow. His steps across the barn floor were slow and muffled. He slid into the shadows and watched the Mole kick his horse into action.

Hanna stopped a few steps from her back door. Her spine tingled from his watchful eyes. She blew out the flame in the lantern and turned to face her assailant. Dark shadows swayed to the night's breeze. She stared into the emptiness. She knew he was there. She could sense his presence, yet her eyes failed to expose him.

Slowly, she moved toward the door. Each backwards step moved her closer to safety. With her hand extended behind her she fumbled for the latch. She entered the house facing the barn. The light from the opened door fell on his shadow as he slipped behind the building. Hanna smiled. Her trap had been set.

Trey spent most of the morning delivering the message to the group. When the last man was charged, he returned to his home. Midnight would come slowly.

Hanna spent the morning preparing her speech. She carefully laid out her plan for the reorganization of the group. If Nathaniel Kristol was going to be stopped, drastic changes needed to be made. Satisfied each detail was flawlessly planned she opened her sister's letter once again. The twisted paper read:

My dear sister,

I am writing with urgency. Our plantation and business are in jeopardy. Two of our most valuable slaves have been missing for eight days. It took Joel many hours of moderate beatings to gather the information needed for their return. They have chosen the same path as George, and I fear they will not return. Lilly insists I grant them freedom, but her husband agrees with me.

It is no secret that the South struggles needlessly in this war effort. We are a strong, resilient people and will not be intimidated by the Yankees' bantering, but we cannot stand idly by and watch our property disappear. It takes many parts to make a whole. I simply will not go without these two men. They are branded as well as tagged bearing our mark of Oak Bend. Their names are Lucas and Elijah.

Please, sister, return them to me.
Camellia

"I promise, Camellia. You will see them restored to your service," she whispered to the paper. "By my dying breath, they will return."

Hanna drummed her fingers. The clock ticked away the hours. Eleven chimes stole her attention from the swinging pendulum. She rose from the table and walked to the back door.

The lantern's light that burned since dusk flickered and went dark. That was her sign. He had arrived and would wait in secret until needed.

She waited until the eleven thirty chime and walked into the dark barn. A soft glow of a rolled cigarette moved through the center of the barn. Hanna tried to shake the feeling of dread, to no avail.

"Are you the first?' she spoke to the cloaked man standing before her.

He drew in a deep breath through his tobacco. The embers licked the edge of the loose paper. Smoke curled out of his nose. His yellowed teeth held the burning butt. No reply came.

Hanna ignored his intimidation tactics. She had endured much worse coming from him. He was unkempt, depreciatory, shifty, and prompt. He was one of the Eradicators and Hanna knew him well. As only one of the two, he was more ruthless.

She lit the flame of the lantern for the second time that evening. The room was filled with shadows. She refused to show any fear or respect toward the conspirator. His purpose of this movement was clearly defined, and she required his attention remain focused. Annoyed with the silence, she turned from him and walked into the center of the room.

183

Hanna crossed her arms and waited. The sounds of the last few chimes of the midnight hour were faintly clear. A smile crossed her face. She removed herself from the waiting ambush and stepped out into the night sky. She walked toward her house.

A loud thump came from the barn. Hanna did not turn around. She opened the back door and picked up a heavy iron rod. The tip left its mark in the dry earth as she pulled it behind her. She stared at the entrance.

Lying on the floor was the lesser Eradicator. A pool of dark blood soaked the sawdust beneath his head. His eyes were fixed on the glowing embers of his assailant's cigarette. Hanna pounded the floor with the rod. The sharpened tip stuck in the wood floor just inches from the man's head. The man did not move.

"How long have you known?" His question punctuated his guilt.

Hanna moved her face close to his and sneered, "I have always known, but I needed you...." She stood and brushed the dust from her hands, "...until now."

Rings of smoke came from beside her. She nodded to him. Her chilled words came without feeling.

"Tidy up this mess." She waved her hands over the dying man. "And tell the men they can come out now."

36

George rode into the Kristol's barn just before sunrise. He was weary from the long night's ride. He placed eight rods before daylight. He was concerned that some would go unnoticed and be misinterpreted as the morning stop. Nathaniel waited silently. George handed him a snippet of paper. The numbers 2 — 17 — 3 stared back at him. He repeated the numbers in his head and lit the edge on fire.

"Twice, I have held these numbers." He wept as the curled orange edges floated to the ground.

"Nathaniel, tonight you should rest." George's tone was assertive.

"No, I must go. Never have the numbers been the same. No. I cannot stand idly by." He rubbed his face with his hands.

Worry covered George's face. Nathaniel eyed him curiously.

"Why so downtrodden?"

George shook his head, "Something is amiss." He rubbed his heart, "I am unsettled." He leaned into his friend. "I feel you should rest tonight."

Nathaniel laughed, "George, we must not allow superstitions to rule our minds. Yes, it is odd to have the same series of numbers come to us. It is natural to relive the horrors that fell on Rebecca when she last held these numbers. But time heals all things and we must continue the fight even without Rebecca's involvement. She yearns for us to continue. I can sense it." Nathaniel turned from George to wipe his eyes.

George listened to his friend's speech. He knew Nathaniel was right, yet he did not have the heart to tell him of Rebecca's continued involvement. Surely he was aware of this.

"What is it, George?"

"Sir, I cannot begin to know your discomfort, yet I have watched you punish yourself and question the acceptance of Rebecca's involvement." He placed his hand on Nathaniel's shoulder. "Her determination fills this house. She has done her best to not stand before you, but...." He lowered his eyes.

"What, George? Please continue."

George gathered the paper's charred remains. "These numbers," he fixed his eyes on Nathaniel's, "were given to me by Rebecca."

"But that is impossible!" he scoffed.

"Nathaniel, I promise you just this afternoon Rebecca gave me these numbers." He lowered his eyes again, "She continues to play her part."

"But...."

"By whom and how she gathers this information is yet a mystery to me. But we met in the clearing. She appeared from town with her loaded wagon. Her smile lights the clearing with or without the rays of the sun. She delivered the numbers. It is not I that traveled into town; she came to me. ”

"This cannot be!" Nathaniel shook his head in disbelief.

"She refuses to yield. '*Until the last slave is freed*' are her words to me. Her smile is wide and her eyes are full of life." Nathaniel sat on the ground and wept. George spoke softly, "I'm sorry, my friend. I thought you knew."

"You must plead with her, George. You must convince her to rest. Others will carry the burden. *I* will carry her burden, *always*."

"There are no words, only notions, and her place has been set. We cannot undo what has been done."

Nathaniel shook his head silently and in disbelief. He knew George's words were true.

Hanna's barn was filled with her group — all but one, and no one questioned his absence. Agitation rumbled through the crowd. Hanna crumpled her sister's letter in her hand. Her tolerance for this band of men had long tired. She slammed the door to capture their attention.

The meeting lasted barely ten minutes. The men had a clear understanding of Hanna's goals. Two slaves would be aboard the nine-thirty train the following evening. One of the Moles was to accompany the Abolitionists to the Kristol house while the rest of the band lay in waiting. The runaways were to be captured and returned to her sister in Georgia. Once safely inside the house the group was to strike and reveal their true intentions. Nathaniel was to be the only one present. The name George was never mentioned.

Hanna labored long over this plan. She was certain to supply each man with a coin and an iron rod, both which would serve as a symbol of belonging to the freedom fighters' movement. When the abolitionists left Nathaniel with the slaves, the Copperheads would strike. Timing was imperative. Nothing could be left to chance. Each detail was laid in stone. Hanna made it clear that if any deviation occurred and a slave was harmed punishment was certain death, by her hand.

The men left her barn in silence. With many missions behind them, this one was laced with urgency. They rode into the darkness carrying the weight of revenge. None avoided the burden. This family matter could not fail.

Grey clouds blanketed the sun. Nathaniel woke much later than normal. He peered out his second-story bedroom window. His eyes were heavy from a restless night. He saw a figure in the distance. It was a woman. She was running.

Suddenly alert he watched her pink dress float in and out of view. The rolling landscape worked as a troublesome cover. He opened the window for a better view. She removed her hat. Her blonde hair brushed her shoulders.

He ran down the back staircase, burst through the kitchen door, and rushed past the barn. George was stacking the logs that he had split. He called to Nathaniel as he ran past the firewood, but Nathaniel did not stop. He ran to the top of the hill and looked in all directions, but she was gone. He called for her. No reply came.

George walked quietly behind his friend. "Was it Rebecca?" Nathaniel nodded.

"I also have seen her."

Hanna woke to a rooster crow. Her body was stiff from yesterday's tension, but her mind was clear. Today was the day her sister's slaves would be captured and returned. She stomped her heel on the floor in defiance.

By eight o'clock that evening Hanna's men had gathered outside of town. Their jaws were tight as they stood in silence. Each was given specific instructions. There was no room for error. Hanna's plan was set in stone; no deviation was permitted.

A lone rider approached the group. His horse was steady in front of the leader. The two spoke in hushed voices.

"All is set. Two slaves are in the seventeenth car. The train is due at nine-thirty."

"And the others?"

"Kristol's men are in place, only one has yet to arrive – the decoy, though his role to us is meaningless."

"How many?"

"Six."

"Including the decoy?"

"Yes, including him."

"Ride! Tonight must be a success," Hanna warned.

He shouted to the group, "Mount up, men!"

One by one the men leapt into their saddles. Dark cloaks covered their bodies; only the rod of freedom was visible.

When the train stopped, they slid into place. Two waited at the end of the train, three on the opposing side, and four hid behind trees along the trail. Only one man was left. He was given specific instructions — kill the wagon driver and assume his position.

Nathaniel and his men waited for the train to slow. Without a word, they moved into place at the seventeenth car. With the sound masked from the dumping coal, Nathaniel broke the lock. Two men jumped from the railcar and followed Nathaniel to the wagon. They slid into the hollowed space.

Nathaniel jumped onto the wagon seat, "Fly!" The driver snapped the reins. A menacing smile covered his cloaked face. The four men disappeared into the darkness.

Trey Cabot sat tall on his horse as he rode down the long lane to Oak Bend. Four of Hanna's men accompanied him. Beaten, blindfolded, and bound together were the two runaway slaves.

The small assembly rode past the north field where a cluster of slaves dug peanuts. The crop harvest was lean, mostly due to the weather, yet the growing absence of many slaves, either from the war or seeking freedom, took a toll on those that remained. All eyes fell on the two who were returning, and their cries rose above the sound of the approaching hooves.

"Lord has mercy!"

"Bes a kind to them, Massa Joel."

"Oh child, Lucas."

"My dear, Elijah needs help."

"Please Massa, find mercy on our brothas."

"Forgive them, Lady Ward!"

"Our brothas has come home."

"Lord, be wif our men."

The cries and wails continued long after Lucas and Elijah had ridden past. The slaves' voices settled into a long gospel song that ushered the men to the front door.

Lilly heard the singing moments before a knock came to the door. She jumped in surprise to see the runaways standing before her. She feared for their punishment, for her mother and husband shared the same anger.

"Do come in," she held out her hand to her guests.

One man stood in the yard with the slaves. He steadied their horse.

She motioned to him. "Please, sir, you also. It is hot. I'll give you a cold drink while you wait for Lady Ward."

He made a motion to tie the horse leaving the men bound together on its back. Lilly shook her head and pointed to the slaves.

"Those men as well."

He was startled at her request but followed. He pulled the battered men from the horse. They stumbled as they tried to stand upright. The shackles from their neck to their feet measured three feet in length. They stood as erect as possible. The man struck their backs with a whip.

"Stand up for the lady!" he mocked.

Lilly's voice was stern. "That is not necessary nor is it tolerated in my presence. Bring in the men as I requested. Do not treat them as animals!" Lilly spun to the angry face of her mother.

"They will not enter my house!" Camellia squealed. "Take them to the yard!"

"But, Mother," Lilly pleaded. "They bear the scars of their disobedience; need they suffer more?"

Camellia could not contain her rage. Her words were desperate, and she was frustrated by her daughter's sympathy. Her finger shook as she pointed to the sweatboxes.

"To the yard and a moderate whipping will *not* do!"

Lilly pleaded with her husband for leniency. He would not yield. He narrowed his eyes and leaned into his wife.

"They must be punished. If we allow this to go unnoticed, how long will it be before others will follow, before others will succeed? Then where would we be? What would become of Oak Bend?"

"We would be a plantation that thrives because of our humanity. Our success would speak for itself. We would be rewarded by our Father in heaven for our righteous ways." She moved closer into him and threw back her hands, "We would be blessed, not cursed." Tears filled her eyes. "You mark my words, Master Joel, if you see this through, you will live to regret it!" She marched down the hall past the kitchen staff that stood wide-eyed and speechless.

Bound together the slaves' bodies were towed through the yard. The taste of the dry earth choked their parched throats as they were chained to the whipping post. Prior to each strike Joel shouted the names of those who had been caught, those that remained as an example, and those that did not survive.

Lilly rushed to the yard. Her hair unfurled and slapped her face as she ran. The sight of her husband wielding the whip made her nauseated. She placed her breathless body between Elijah and the strap.

The motion could not be halted. The whip stuck her torso and wrapped around her back. She winced at the sharp, unexpected pain. The back of her dress was torn open. Blood splattered on Elijah's face and soaked the fabric. She crumpled to the ground from the single lash.

The sight before him paralyzed Joel. His wife's cameo skin ripped open by his hand. He turned from her and vomited.

Lilly lay motionless on the ground. Fire ran through her body. The saturated cotton felt cool on her wounds but offered no relief. Joel crept to her side, begging for forgiveness. She managed to stand without his aid.

"Untie them. They have suffered enough," she whispered.

Joel tried to help her, but she dismissed his efforts. He walked beside her with his arm outstretched as an offering of assistance. Even through a forward stumble she refused his help.

Her eyes narrowed as she spoke. "Today, the brutality stops."

"I did not...."

"No!" she shouted. Her body spun from the pain. "You will *never*! By my wounds you will forever be reminded."

She turned from him and walked through the door. One of the housemaids took her arm. Tears decorated the maid's face as she disapprovingly eyed her master.

Joel spoke no more. He tossed the whip on the porch floor and hung his head. The screams of his mother-in-law filled his ears. He walked to the men and unlocked the shackles.

Silence greeted the trio as Joel helped the slaves to their shack. Warm water and clean cloths sat on the floor inside the doorframe. The pungent smell of a fresh herb poultice burned his nostrils. Two women stood, heads bowed and silent, while Joel helped the men to their cots. One woman placed a tightly wrapped cloth in Joel's hand. He left their hovel without a word.

The smell of the homemade medicine followed Joel into the manor and up the back staircase to their bedroom. Lilly lay face down on a white sheet. It was speckled red. He gave the poultice to the upstairs maid and watched as she cleaned and dressed his wife's wounds.

It was then he realized that Lilly's complaints of brutality were sound. He tried to recall the number of slaves that he had beaten over the years but could not. He tried to remember their names or how badly their wounds looked when he was finished with their punishment. He hung his head in shame and knelt beside his wife.

Her eyes met his. Joel moved his mouth to speak but was unable to form the words. Lilly lifted her hand and touched his cheek. She knew his thoughts; there was no need to speak.

Camellia rebuked her son-in-law until her voice was drowned by the screams inside his head. He was unable to focus on her words yet understood her accusations. Joel had permanently marked his wife. Their relationship would not remain unscathed. He would be reminded each time Lilly bathed, undressed, or spoke. He knew. He understood. Never again would he hold a whip.

George wiped his face with the back of his hand. The sadness he felt would not be comforted. He chastised himself for not following his feeling. He should have accompanied Nathaniel in the wagon. He knew in his heart the minute the buckboard moved from his sight that all would change. He sensed the destruction. He could not shake the guilt. He clung to the marker and cried.

Rebecca hung in the shadows. She too was full of emotion but did not offer comfort to George. She held a gathering of pink roses and lingered for the opportunity to be alone with her father.

George remained for nearly an hour. When his tears dried and he could offer no more, he jumped on the back of his mare. In his final returned glance he saw Rebecca. It was the only notion that forced a smile.

Rebecca timidly approached her father's resting place. She placed her hands on his stone. It was fashioned like her mother's. Its plain inscription made her cry. It read:

Nathaniel Kristol
October 1864

39

After the fall of Atlanta on September 2, 1864, news of the war created heightened awareness in Salem. By October major portions of the railroad were destroyed in the Confederates' attempt to sever the Union supply line. Due to the interruptions fewer slaves came by way of rail.

During this brief period several new safe houses were established along the broken lines. Veiled traveling time was lengthened by over two weeks, and many slaves were apprehended and returned to their plantations. For an individual to pass through Salem by way of the rail system grew rarer by the week.

After Abraham Lincoln's defeat of Democratic candidate George McClellan in the November 1864 election, the North seemed to breathe more easily. Although the tension between the Union and Confederate armies continued to escalate over the issue of slavery, Lincoln became more convinced that emancipation was not only evident it was necessary.

By mid-November William Tecumseh Sherman began his "March to the Sea." Two starved Union soldiers who escaped the Confederate war camp of Andersonville accidentally stumbled into Sherman's camp, and their emaciated state fueled Sherman's fire of accountability. He was determined to make the South pay for these atrocities and within a week destroyed their rail supply line between Dalton and Atlanta. By December 21, 1864, his troops occupied Savannah.

It was during this flurry that the flow of runaway slaves had noticeably increased. Most came by foot though a few were smuggled by way of the train. Seldom did three days pass before George heard a knock on the Kristols' door or saw a note scribbled with three simple numbers. Several times the Slave Catchers arrived at the home only to be surprised when a black man answered the door. After a quick show of appropriate paperwork and several additional letters from Lilly, the men were satisfied.

Most times, the men assumed that George was misinterpreted to be a slave and left without a further search. Only once did they insist to enter the home. His guard never lessened nor his breath expelled until the group of perpetrators left the property.

The calm of mid-winter evenings seemed the loneliest. Darkness filled the sky before the evening chores had begun. Many of those nights, sleep came easily and early.

The clock chimed eight in the dining room. It's clear numbered bells rang throughout the house. George finished the last bit of beef stew for a meager dinner. He had been sixteen days without a slave. The break seemed eerily haunting.

His tired feet carried him through the dining room. He smiled at Rebecca's bouquet that graced the center of the table. It had been several weeks since she visited. He continued up the stairs to the second window, lit a candle, sent a silent prayer to Mim, and crawled into bed.

He woke to Rebecca's desperate face just inches from his. She spoke in hushed urgent tones as she waved a snippet of paper.

"George! George, you must come." She placed the paper into his hands. "It is late, and word was just given to me."

George sat up in his bed and looked at the numbers 2 —17 — 3. He swallowed the bitter memory.

"Tonight?" came his stunned reply.

"Yes. It is late."

The sound of the nine o'clock chime rang through the house. George threw off his covers and pulled his work clothes from the hook. His words were frantic as he rushed to dress.

"But, Miss Rebecca, it is too late to call for others."

"Yes, George, you must go alone. The wagon waits."

Dread crept into his mind. These numbers have come to him twice before and both times were met with a tragedy. He jumped onto Rebecca's wagon.

She stood before him dressed in a thin cotton dress. She was neither covered with a wrap nor bothered by the frigid temperatures. She touched the back of his hand and smiled.

"All is well, George. Your ride will bring you much joy."

He snapped the reins, and the horse headed down the well-trodden path. He ran with speed of urgency. George checked his pocket watch that Lacey had gifted to him many years earlier. He had only seventeen minutes to reach the tracks. His eyes fell on the written numbers several times and sought comfort in Rebecca's words. He wrestled to cast off the anxiety.

The false bottom buckboard bounced along the snowy path. Many times the drifting snow should have hindered their passage, but they moved through it with ease. George felt he was riding to his destiny, and it felt like doom.

He rounded the final corner of the trail just as the train sounded its arrival. How he traveled so far so quickly was a mystery, yet he was glad to arrive unscathed.

He placed his rod on the lock of the seventeenth cattle car and waited for the rattle of the dispersing coal. When the sounds rang in his ears he snapped the lock. He gasped at the faces before him. It was Mim and Monroe.

They ran to the wagon and forced their bodies into the cover of the false bottom. The horse jumped into action before George settled into the seat. The sound of the moving train calmed his nerves until the woods echoed the slamming of the door.

Panic ran through his veins. In his excitement to see these familiar faces he had forgotten to close the railcar door. He knew the unmistakable bang would spring the Watchers into action. His safe passage was fated.

"Brace yourselves," he yelled over the wind. "Company is upon us!"

George snapped the reins forcing the horse to his limit. The extra weight in the wagon proved taxing, but he did not falter. In the distance George saw the woods, which stood just beyond his property line. He prayed for protection.

Mim and Monroe's bodies jostled in the narrow space. Monroe struggled to reach the contents in his pocket. With Mim's help they gathered all twenty of the six pointed lead stars.

George's voice rang clear as they passed the property line. His horse was wild with foam but showed no sign of tiring. He let his guard relax at the sight of the house. The lone candle burned brightly in the window. He smiled at the thought of bringing Mim to this place. He thanked Rebecca for her diligence and relaxed his grip on the reins.

From his left peripheral vision two riders appeared with their horses in fierce pursuit. George yelled in surprise. He fumbled to regain control. His cries of certain defeat were clear.

Monroe dropped one iron star after another through a hole created by a shrunken knot. It was difficult to maneuver in the cramped quarters but he managed to force all but one star in the path of the riders. The loose star rattled by their feet while they bounced through the snow-covered field.

The iron stars wedged in the center of the horse's hooves and caused the animals to rear in pain. One rider and horse tumbled to the ground and rolled until they rested on the opposite sides of the trail. The rider's body was crushed from the weight of his horse and settled into an awkward position.

His companion slowed and jumped to the ground. He stepped on an iron star and twisted his ankle. Cursing sounded through the empty field. He hobbled to his friend's limp body.

The distraction ensured the trio's safety. George drove the wagon into the barn and yelled to Mim and Monroe to follow him. Proper cover of their footprints in the snow was a luxury he could not entertain. He led them up the back staircase into the paneled passageway. Once secure, he ran back down the steps and out the back door. His face flooded with awe at what he saw — not a single print was visible in the snow. His flight had been covered.

He lifted his eyes toward the barn and smiled. Rebecca stood in the doorway. Her cotton dress moved gracefully in the wind. She waved to help celebrate his success. Life and love had found her friend.

George heard Lacey's voice in his head. He nodded and whispered, "Yes. I, George, am free from slavery." He turned to the angry sound of pounding on his front door.

40

George woke in a cold sweat. The sky was still dark. He listened to the sound of the tall case's pendulum. Its rhythm brought no comfort. He replayed the night's events in his mind.

He remembered the sound of the pounding at his front door. Expecting the ritual of surprise and accusations as he stood before a white man, he was stunned when no proof was necessary. The man who stood before him he did not know, yet he recognized George. The thought unnerved him.

His escalated tone would not be silenced until George moved him through the house. Satisfied no slave was present, he insisted on viewing the barn. When George hesitated, he became enraged.

"What are you hiding?"

"I assure you, sir, I am not."

"Then show me your barn!"

George pulled on his boots in silence. He gathered his coat and tossed it over his shoulders. The glowing absence of footprints in the snow should have been evidence enough, but this man was insistent. George swallowed hard as he slid the barn door open. He did not have time to hide the rod, groom and secure his horse, or store the wagon in its proper place. When he opened the door, he was astounded.

The barn was in perfect order. George's horses were in their individual stalls; some rested, others fed. The glaring absence of a wagon left the man speechless.

His tone changed from accusatory to apologetic. "We were in pursuit of a man in a wagon."

George gathered his senses and responded, "We?"

The man hung his head. "Yes, two of us followed a freedom fighter, an abolitionist. We were certain he was harboring a slave. We followed him to the edge of your property and then…," he lowered his voice, "…my comrade…uhhh…stumbled."

"Where is he now?"

"His body lies just beyond your property. He struggles to breathe."

"You abandoned him?" George was mortified.

"Naught could be done." The man stared into the empty barn. He walked toward the door. "My apologies for the intrusion."

George nodded, "Accepted."

He watched the rider disappear over the knoll in the front field. He turned in circles, his eyes scanning the barn for the wagon, but it was not there. A flood of nerves rushed over him — Was this a dream?

He moved through the swirling snow with little hindrance. He needed to see Mim's face. He needed to be certain he wasn't dreaming.

The following morning Monroe and George laughed as he relayed his story. Mim smiled with obvious affection. It was then she was certain her road had ended. She had survived a return to George, and she was determined to stay, no matter the cost.

Mim prepared a hearty breakfast with George at her side. Each request was met with a means — a skillet, firewood, lard, and eggs. They sat together at the square kitchen table until the sun was high in the sky.

George was startled by a thump that settled against the side door. He pulled his pocket watch from his pants. It was ten minutes before high noon. Mim noticed the grave look on his face.

"George?"

After a slight hesitation, he answered, "Yes?"

"Why are you drawn?"

"The sound at the door is a liberty call. Tomorrow at noon another man desiring freedom will pass through Salem on the railroad. An iron rod stands against the funeral door as a sign of which train he will be traveling. With the coming of the noon hour the rod tells of the time of the freedom ride." The tall case rang twelve. "Tomorrow I must go to help another brother find his way. He may be with us for a night, or he may stay with another. Details will come in the glen two hours before."

Monroe's response as a surprise, "Can Isa help?"

"You need to stay here and hidden until your freedom path is decided. Tomorrow I will have all answers. Until then I will relish your company."

41

George stood behind the cover of a large beech tree. The snow had begun to melt and traveling was easy. His heart fluttered.

By ten o'clock all of the men had gathered. George made no mention of his last minute ride the night prior.

Nathaniel's absence was never more profound than when the riders gathered in the glen. He had been their leader and orchestrated their well-designed plans. His death cast a constant shadow on the assembly. George found it difficult to speak, not as the only black man, but as one who longed for his friend.

A small piece of paper was passed from man to man. With numbers solidified in their minds, the men rose to the sound of the freedom call. They rode through the snow in single file to conceal their numbers. They took their places and waited for the train.

No matter how often this ritual was followed the level of danger did not decrease. Although the evening provided visual cover, its swiftness was impeded by the same benefit, and the noon peril was exposed by daylight. Truth be told, George disliked the noon raids more. He was edgy until the railcar door was closed and relieved that his part at least for today had ended. He watched a single pregnant woman ride toward Unserheim.

Thoughts of Mim shadowed his return. Emotions flowed through him; anxiety, excitement, tiredness, and finally rejuvenation. He passed through field and glen without any recollection. When the house came into view, his heart jumped.

It was past three o'clock when George stumbled into the kitchen. The house was eerily quiet. He dared not shout out names for fear of unwanted guests, so his stealthy moves went unnoticed. The only sound he heard was his heart thumping in his ears.

He took the center hall stairs one at a time, avoiding the fourth due to its creak. He walked with his back against the wall unaware his hands were fixed on his iron rod. He entered each bedroom inspecting every corner, every closet, but no one was found.

Finally satisfied that he was alone, he walked into the raised paneled hallway, slid the one panel from its place, and crawled into the narrow passageway that led to the hiding place. He knocked on the door. Relief came with the opening of the inside lock. The only one present was Mim. Her face was stained with tears.

"What has happened? Where is Monroe?"

"We heard a knock on the door. I was paralyzed with fear. Monroe ordered me to the hiding place. After he was certain I was safe, he answered the call." She lowered her voice. "I heard muffled sounds, yet I could not understand. There were no angry voices, no shouting. I waited but only heard silence. I entered this room just shy of one o'clock."

"It is half past three." George, filled with questions, was conflicted — he was happy to see Mim but anxious for what had become of Monroe. Many questions rattled his thoughts, but he was drawn into Mim's blue eyes. After much deliberation he extended his hand.

"Come. Come with me."

After crawling through the duct, they continued down the hallway until it met the front staircase. He led Mim to the highest room in the house. It resembled a lookout room graced with windows on all four sides. A lone chair and table sat in the center of the room.

Mim drew in her breath but refused to exhale. They stood one story above the roofline. The view in all directions was unobstructed but for one large oak.

"Nearly all can be seen."

She knew what he was saying, but her heart refused comfort. Her smile was thin. "What can be seen? It has been two hours since silence filled this home."

They looked out each window and followed the multiple tracks with their eyes. George felt helpless.

"Where shall I go? Which trail should I follow?"

Mim's desperate gaze moved from east to south, south to west, west to north, and then returned to the east. She collapsed in George's arms.

"Give me my path," he pleaded.

"I know naught what to say. His absence is puzzling, but my heart feels no evil has fallen on him."

"Nonetheless, I will search."

George left Mim in the windowed room. She watched George lead his horse on all trails. Once he decided his path, he waved to Mim and disappeared into the snow.

Mim waited for several hours in that room until the restlessness over took her. She needed to occupy her mind with anything other than worry.

She walked down the hall to a small sewing room in the west corner. She rummaged through a needlepoint box and selected several colors of dyed flax. No matter if the shade were pale or vibrant, it would satisfy her mind. She unrolled her sampler from her knapsack and carried her items back to the viewpoint.

She separated the strings by color and arranged each strand from light to dark. She pulled the longest green fiber from the table, threaded it, and began to sew. She had finished the border in the train. It resembled a vine of strawberries, still green from early development; only a few of the berries held a blush of color, for Mim only had one thread of red. She smiled at the four red fibers that lay on the table before her.

The silk cloth used for the background was finely made. The weave was tight and made counting difficult, but Mim had excelled in stitchery while attending finishing school. Her long fingers moved the threads with ease. Soon the words of her verse were near complete:

Wisdoms ways are ways of pleasantness
and all her paths are peace.
I love them that love me and those that seek
me early shall find me.

She finished the verse in the dusk's failing light. She stared into the growing darkness as she had hundreds of times in the past two hours. The clock chimed six. Winter, darkness, and the dread of this night would soon end. She heard rustling and watched two men on one horse come in the opposite direction of George's departure.

She pressed her face against the black window praying for it to be George and Monroe. If her wish had been mistaken and she lingered too long, her revealing would be certain, but with her face lit with excitement, she recognized the men. She ran down the stairs to greet them.

Monroe filled the evening with his tales of adventure. He explained that the men who came to the door were abolitionists. They mistook Monroe for George. He rode with them to the meeting in the glen. He witnessed first-hand the inner workings of the movement. Overwhelmed with the sense of duty, he was about to reveal himself when George rode into the clearing.

The group's tone moved from sober to celebration after George told his tale. He explained he rode alone, was pursued, and nearly overcome. He mentioned all but Rebecca. Monroe showed the men his lead star.

"What is this?" The men passed the small, but weighty object to one another.

"The souf yousa them, suh. Trip up the union hawses."

"Where did you find them?"

"Isa picked `em up on the way. Thot they jus may come in handy and sure nuf did." The men laughed.

"How many do you have?"

"I had twenty of `em but toss `em all on the groun through a hole in the wagon." He held up the six-pointed star. "This ones too big."

The men discussed the possible use of these objects at length. They debated the dangers of traveling alone and chastised George for his attempt.

"The outcome could have been fatal."

George hung his head. "I could not ignore the call." He looked at each man with intent as he finished. "None standing before me now would have lingered in the safety of their home when a life depended on them alone. It was a decision that was made out of duty. It has not been long since I sat in that railcar awaiting my freedom." He lowered his voice. "What if you had ignored the rod? Where would I be? Captured and most likely dead. I owe my life to you. How else can I repay that debt but to do it for others?"

"George, we are not debating your valor. We are simply stating the danger of a solo flight."

"There was no time."

"Who brought you this news so late?" the man asked those present. A murmur of 'not I' and 'nor I' moved through the glen. "Who then, George? Did you not fear a trap was laid?"

This was the question George feared. These men had moved through many more missions than George. They had tasted death in their circle of comrades more than most. They knew of the tale of Rebecca and Nathaniel.

"I did not fear of a trap. My trust is solid in her."

"Her?"

"It was Rebecca."

42

Monroe and Mim stayed with George for three weeks. During that time the abolitionists devised a plan for their continuance. They decided the best route was the rail to New York and on to Canada from there. They felt it was best to avoid Michigan and its lure of safety to stay. Monroe agreed, but Mim was anxious. George was silent.

Each day the bond between George and Mim grew. They sat together in evenings long after Monroe had fallen asleep and rose early for the morning chores.

Monroe began to fear that he would be continuing to Canada alone. He woke early to speak with his sister. Mim was awake when Monroe sat on the edge of her bed. Her eyes were puffy from the night's tears.

Monroe whispered, "You wants to stay, Mim?"

She sobbed on her brother's shoulders, "I fear for you traveling alone, but my heart wants to remain."

"But what 'bout yous freedom?"

"I will be as safe here as in Canada."

"Isa douts that," Monroe's words were woven with sarcasm.

"Much of my time is consumed with these thoughts. I know the day is upon us when we must go, but I wish to remain with George."

"Has he ax you to stay?"

Mim nodded her head, "Many times."

"And whats do yous say?"

"I have told him that I needed to think on these things. I said I must discuss it with you."

"Souns like yous dun made up yous mind to me."

"Oh, Monroe, do not be angry with me. I am riddled with guilt, as I fear for your safety. What if something happens to you?"

"Mim, Isa be fine. Nuttin's gonna happen to me. Isa knew when Isa see yous two togetha. Yous shuld stay. Yous belong wif each otha." He lowered his head, "Isa jus wish yousa tell me befo now."

"Yet you knew."

"Yessa Ma'am."

"Shall we talk to George together?"

"Isa rekon we shuld."

When they walked down the back staircase, George sat at the table. He held his head in his hands.

"George?" Mim quietly sat beside him. "Monroe and I have something to tell you."

George's eyes pleaded for his desired response. He nodded and waited for her to continue.

"We spoke this morning. I told Monroe of our conversations. I expressed my desire to stay here with you." George began to smile. "He said he thinks we belong together."

"You will stay then?" he asked timidly.

"If you will have me, George, I would like to stay."

He jumped from his chair, and it toppled to the floor in a crash. He threw his arms around Mim and kissed her. Monroe smiled from across the room.

"Now listen to me, George. My sista is pure. I `spect her to stay that way or Isa not lettin' her stay."

Surprised, but tickled by his comment he burst into laughter. Monroe and Mim quickly joined him. The three stood together with their arms wrapped in a circle.

Breakfast conversation was light and festive. It was Tuesday, the day George worked for Daniel. He lingered a bit longer than normal and set off long after sunrise. A thin layer of ice had formed over the melting snow making the ride to Unserheim a noisy one. George rehearsed his speech so many times his horse seemed to snort in compliance. His heart was warm.

Daniel's strike of hot iron on his anvil echoed down the street. George slid from his mare and followed into sequence. Daniel's eyes never left his work.

"You are a bit late this morning, Mr. George."

George smiled at his comment, "I was delayed."

"By design?"

"By desire."

"So what is the plan?"

"Wedding tomorrow?"

Daniel did not hesitate. He was aware of George's feelings for Mim. "Have you visited the parson?"

"I hoped we could do that together."

"That we could," Daniel eyed George, "when we finish our work."

"My expectations would be that."

"Do you have a ring?"

"No sir. We will have to do without."

"And what of a location?"

"My thoughts were a quiet ceremony at the house."
Daniel nodded and smiled.

"What is your opinion?"

"My thoughts do not matter. The law is against a free man being bonded to a slave, but my hope is slavery will be abolished and it will not matter. Mim would acquire your rights to the Kristol property through your union." He swallowed hard. "Nathaniel would be honored." He placed his hand on George's shoulder. "Fill your home with many children — many free children. God is smiling on you, my friend."

"Your words are a comfort. My only fear is exposure."

"Naught from my lips or those of my household."

George wiped the sweat from his brow and smiled. "God is smiling on *you*, my friend."

The men worked quickly. They refused to stop for lunch even through Margaret's insistence. With the last forged iron piece settled into place, Daniel excused himself.

After a brief conversation with Margaret, he returned.

"Shall we go?"

"I am ready."

The men rode to the minister's home. After a lengthy discussion he conceded to perform the ceremony in secret. Daniel thought it should be private with only Monroe as a witness to avoid suspicion from the Copperheads.

"Before you depart I once again must stress my apprehension. It is clearly outside of the law and the rules of the Quakers, but I answer to the One who lives above us all, and my heart is urging my involvement when my mind is screaming contradiction." His gruff expression softened. He looked at George. "I will come alone at the noon hour."

"Thank you, sir," was all George could manage. Joy choked his throat.

He also thanked Daniel many times before riding home. Daniel assured George his decision was just.

"This brings me to one last pronouncement, George. There is no debate in this matter." His face was stern. "Your absence is necessary for Monroe's flight."

"But...." Daniel held up his hand.

"No debate! Your duty will be with your new wife. She should not sit alone, wondering of your safety."

"I...." Daniel again raised his hand.

"You will remain with Mim! Monroe will be in very capable hands. I will send a rider to deliver the message of his safe passage, when it is prudent. The good people of the freedom houses are to send word of his crossing. You will know of his journey through their unwritten words."

"Unwritten words?" George questioned.

"It is perilous for the letters to be specific in nature. Often they are opened, read, and resealed. They will arrive with only remnants of the wax seal. So there will be no mention of Monroe, his well-being, or his safety. You will know he has passed from one house to the next simply by receiving a letter of unrelated news. Any attempt to mention the mission would be known by the Copperheads, and their reaction would be swift. Find comfort in the receipt of the letter."

"As a sign, not through the words?"

"Yes. Some are craftier than others and their words can be revealed through a solution of water and vinegar. Some do not have this ink, so they align the covert words vertically. Still most will simply send a letter about their harvest, family, or simply local news. In those letters the news is in the receipt of the paper itself. Do you understand?"

"I do." George was stunned at Daniel's words. The unity in movement and the secreted objects – iron rods, bonnet colors, candles, coins, newspapers, and now letters some with special ink astounded him.

His eyes filled with tears. "I have no words, only gratitude."

Daniel grinned, "One final notion." He extended his hand to George. His fist was down turned and closed. George opened his palm, and in it Daniel placed a gold band.

"It was Margaret's when she was younger. Her fingers have grown and it no longer fits. It is our desire to entrust it to Mim."

George slipped the wide gold band over the tip of his little finger. It barely moved past his first knuckle. It was graced with fine carvings of flowers and vines and monogrammed with a scripted *M*.

George's eyes welled. Words were difficult. "I am honored," was all that would come.

Daniel nodded in silent agreement. George settled into the saddle but turned to face his friend. He made no attempt to hide his emotions.

"Tomorrow will be a fine day. God speed, George." He waved as George rode toward home.

43

im woke giddy with excitement. Nerves kept her from breakfast. Her fingers were busy with the final stitches of her dress. It was a simple white cotton silhouette, one she had worn before but with a few added embellishments.

The day of Monroe's disappearance, Mim found a box of fabric — pieces of velvet, silk, cotton, and lace. After George's approval, she separated the lace and selected four pieces to attach to the bottom of her dress. She hand-stitched a gathering of white flowers with pearled buttons for the center in the fashion of her sampler training. The morning of her wedding day, she added a single white dove to the cross-stitched scene. This signified the presence and flight of her brother.

She placed the dress on her bed and smoothed out the fabric. She was pleased with the adornments. Her thoughts were interrupted by a quiet knock on the door.

"It is bad luck to see the bride before it is time."

"But Isa not the groom," Monroe teased.

She opened the door and wrapped her arms around her brother. He held a plate of eggs, a slice of crusty bread, and an apple.

"George says yous mus eat sommen."

"Come sit with me, Monroe." She patted the edge of her bed. "Let us plan your tomorrow."

"George says he's been ordered to stay wif yous."

"He is staying here?"

"That's what mista Daniel says. Mista Daniel says enuf men to sees me off safe. George needs to be wif you, his new wife."

"I still chill at the word."

Monroe danced around the room, "Wife...wife...new wife."

"Settle now. Nerves are not welcomed on a wedding day."

They spoke about his travel and the chosen path he would take. Mim made Monroe admit his nerves, but she mostly helped him express his dreams. They spoke of freedom, love, and family. They dreamed of reuniting as free siblings and watching their families grow together.

Her nimble fingers twisted silk threads through a square of sheer fabric as they spun their dreams. When she finished her veil, the tall case chimed eleven. Her untouched food laid waiting, but the desire was not in her. Monroe excused himself so she could dress.

She smiled at her brother as he walked through the door. His speech was not polished, but he walked with the pride of a free man. She whispered a silent prayer of protection for his journey. He blew her a kiss and walked down the front staircase.

Ten minutes before the noon hour she stood alone in the tower room. She watched a lone rider approach and knew her time as a single woman was growing thin. Her heart fluttered when she counted the chimes once again from the clock. She began her three-floor descent.

When she stepped on the first landing, she saw a single white lily placed on the banister. She wrapped both hands around her present and drew in its fragrance. She did not recall when her feet left the staircase. She heard Monroe's clear voice. He sang a Southern gospel song. The tune was familiar, yet the words were special for today. She entered the front receiving room. Three men grinned — though the widest smile was George's.

Mim's white dress followed each curve of her body. The lace ruffles danced with each step. Her smooth hair was pulled to one side and wrapped with strings of silk. George extended his hand to her. It was then he noticed the lily.

The ceremony lasted only a few minutes. The simple promise to bind themselves to each other was repeated in the normal fashion. George presented the gold band to Mim. Her face mirrored his excitement. He slipped it on her finger with little difficulty and whispered his promise to her. When they kissed, he felt he had been given life's sweetest gift. He smiled at his bride.

After brief tears and long hugs, the parson rode back into town. George presented his wife with a fresh pot of rabbit stew, turnips, onion, potatoes, and apples. Monroe joined them in the feast but began to feel anxious about the upcoming event. It would be a long day until the nine-thirty train. He excused himself from the table.

Mim fingered the petals of the lily and invited George to enjoy its fragrance.

"Thank you, my husband, for this beautiful day, for the ceremony, the ring, and the flower."

George grinned at her words until her mention of the flower. "I did all but the lily."

She looked at him puzzled. "It was resting on the banister and begged to come with me." She giggled, "It was not from you?"

"Lilies do not grow in the winter."

"Not this far north," she mused.

George smiled. He knew who brought it.

44

Hidden by the cover of darkness, Monroe slipped from the property. Mim promised she would not show sorrow but in the end could not conform. She watched the band of shadows move along the row of pine trees that bordered the property until they were swallowed by the gloom. George held her as she cried.

The white lily stood proud in its vase as they sat silently at the table. George watched Mim flip the pages of a book though he knew her mind did not capture its words. The clock struck eleven.

"We should have word soon," he tried to be reassuring. Mim offered no response.

After another thirty minutes they heard a quiet rap at the back door. George jumped at the sound and rushed to invite the news. A tall man cloaked in black slid through the doorway.

"All is well. We found no opposition."

"That is great news." George offered with a wide smile. Mim's silent tears mimicked his sentiment. George held out his hand. "Thank you for your diligence and speed."

The young man offered a quick tale of their uneventful ride. When he finished, he added, "All will go as planned.

Monroe is in capable hands. Many have traveled along this same path to freedom. Trust that he will find the way to freedom and pray our country will abolish this atrocity soon." He tipped his head and slipped out of the door.

"I feel as if I can breathe with this news." Mim whispered, "I am exhausted."

"Sleep will come easy on this night."

George seemed to snore before his head settled into his pillow. Mim was mentally spent, but her mind would not allow rest. She tried to find a comfortable position in her new bed. With each move George inched a bit closer until she felt nearly forced off the mattress. She got up and walked into the kitchen.

Her mind wandered to her mother. She wept for the sorrows in her life, for her children born and taken from her, sold into a life of hardship and hatred for financial gain. She tried to recall the number of children but could not.

The baby she remembered most was her sister. She was born when Mim was thirteen. She was premature and struggled often to breathe. Mim was instructed to gently lift her and pat her back if her breathing ceased. If that did not cause her to take a breath, she was to gently shake her. Mim remembered following those orders several times in a few hours.

She was a beautiful baby graced with long slender fingers and toes much like her own. Though her body was extremely thin, she measured nineteen inches in length. Her eyes were wide and bright with a haze of blue. She was a quiet child and a stubborn eater. She only remained with her mother for ten days.

Mim often wondered if the baby lived, if she had received the care needed, if she remembered to breathe, or if she missed her family. She was Mim's only sister and she knew nothing of her.

She slid into the opposite side of the bed without a stir from George. His snores had changed to slow deep breaths and helped her to fall asleep. She woke to the sound of clanking dishes.

It was three weeks before the first letter arrived. Mim crowded George as he read the words aloud:

Dearest brother,

The days have been long and nights longer as this dreadful weather seems to cling to us unwanted. The sun had shone its yellow face only a few times this month withholding its warmth from the ice of the Hudson River. We have managed to keep a few holes open to fish, yet its yield is less than slim. We long for the busy days of spring, the warmth of the sun, the rushing of melting water to the sea, and for the robust movement of our water trade routes. It has been a long, lean winter.

We have received word from the Whitacre family that two of their sons have been wounded in the war. They are traveling separate paths toward home. The road is long and rough, for their wounds are great, but their pace is slow yet steady and will be welcomed by the entire town upon their return. John is expected to arrive within two weeks and Sid will soon follow. I will relay your wishes for a safe return.

My heart is light as I write to you. I long for the days that family can once again be together to laugh and love. I long for the fragrance of Mother's recipes of trout with spring greens, and a loaf of fresh baked bread finished with a generous slice of rhubarb pie. In those days our memories are relished for the taste to linger through the days of June.

I am trusting your health is strong and your skies clearer for hearing from your sister on this day.

All my love,
Sarah

After both read the letter twice Mim asked, "Do you think Monroe is hurt?"

"I know not. This form of secrecy opens the door for frustration." George shook his head, "If he is wounded, it is clear he has passed from his first location toward the next."

"I trust your thoughts are true. I will force the negative thoughts from taking up residence and continue to pray for his safety."

"It is all we can do. He is in capable hands, Mim. We must believe all will go as planned."

Nearly two months had passed since Monroe's flight began before a second letter came to the family. The couple read the words together and was filled with more angst than with the first. It read:

My dear cousin,

I write to you in a bit of a quandary. I am faced with the need to liquidate some property. Some of my cattle suffered greatly from the hard winter, yet my means to fatten them before market are meager. I know not if I can count on you for financial support so my farm will not suffer and my reputation be restored.

In haste,
Chester

George stared at the words on the parchment. Mim sat in tired silence beside him.

"I have read these words yet I know not of what they say." Mim's voice quivered.

George cleared his throat, "Daniel explained some are better than others in hiding their intentions."

"But this letter has no defining factors, no location, or reassurance, only desperation and suffering." Her eyes pleaded for answers, "Oh, George, I fear the worst."

He wrapped his arms around his wife. "We must find comfort in the receipt of the letters — those were the words from Daniel. We will not always know. Comfort must come with the news. Monroe is moving. He has moved through two safe houses." He lifted her face and kissed her moistened cheeks, "Monroe is moving."

Mim forced destructive thoughts from forming the rest of the day. She found George staring at the letter several times. He too strayed from irreversible ideas. He busied his day in the barn feeding his own cattle and contemplating the words of the letter.

The evening found them hearthside warmed by a robust fire. The flames licked the brick and colored them with soot. Mim and George rocked silently. The smell of the bubbling stew filled the air.

Mim used the poker to swing the crane and cast iron kettle toward her. With a heavy cloth she lifted the lid and announced dinner. She placed the footed pot on the hearth and dished up two large portions of simmering vegetables.

George stared at the letter as he ate. Suddenly he lunged forward. His voice was hopeful.

"Mim!" His thick fingers pointed to the words at the end of each line. "Look at this!" He repeated the words to her, "Need suffered yet are so restored."

She mimicked his discovery, "Need suffered, yet are so restored." She threw her arms around her husband's neck and spilled the contents of her bowl. "That is great news! Monroe's needs suffered but are restored. He *was* wounded and he is healing!" She placed her hand over her heart and sighed, "My brother is fine. Thank you, Lord."

By mid-spring three more letters had arrived — two from New York and the final one from Canada. Monroe had made it. Mim read the final letter to her husband.

My brother,

It is with great joy I write to you with news. Our son has arrived though we are conflicted with his name. It is not unlike your sister-in-law to find humor in a tense situation. He came with a bit of difficulty and in the process lost his left hand, but all else is perfect. His disposition is bright and his face is lit with hope. It is only his name that puzzles us. Emily would like to follow in the tradition of our other children but I offer only opposition. After Mark, Matthew, Mary, Martha and Melba, I tire of the sentiment. I am clinging to the hope for the name George, after my only brother. What say you?

In long celebration,
Michael

Mim danced around her husband. Rays of joy covered her face. "My brother is free! Monroe is free!" Her words came in song.

By late autumn Mim had begun to show a protruding belly. She counted the days and credited her excitement of Monroe's freedom to the source.

"If it is a boy, what shall he be named?"

George thought for a moment and answered, "Monroe."

"Not your name sake?"

"George was the name given to me by Lady Ward. My memory of my true name is lost. Many times I have tried to recall the sound of my mother's voice calling to me but cannot. The name George has sufficed, but it is not my true self."

"Then, Monroe it is." Mim agreed, "And if it is a girl?"

"Hmmm," George rubbed his whiskered chin. "On that I need to think. What are your thoughts?"

"I have none that are important."

George stared at his beautiful wife. Her light skin, smooth brown hair, and blue eyes were traits from her father, but her grace and sensitivity were that of her mother.

"What brings a smile?"

"I was thinking about three important girls, those that sacrificed for my freedom."

"Lilly and Lacey?"

"And Rebecca."

"And for our little one?"

"On that I am conflicted. All were beautiful, brave, defiant, and compassionate. They seemed to have been born of a similar mold, though two were clearly not. Without them I would not be with you today. We would not be in this house, on this property, living as freed slaves. Our paths would not have crossed." George shook his head at his words. "We would not be and neither would our child."

"Does that help with a decision?"

"It complicates it." He kissed Mim's palm, "We have a bit of time before a name must be decided. Let us think on this."

Days turned to weeks and weeks to months. The autumn's harvest had long been settled and winter had reared its ugly head. For Mim, the long quiet January evenings were welcomed.

George's freedom calls became less frequent since Mim's pregnancy. She lived as a free slave, yet her master had not yet granted her liberty. The appropriate money and letter had been delivered in September though no word had returned. Her letter had either not been delivered or had caused a search to ensue. Although she did not speak of her apprehension, she prayed it was the former.

Mim rubbed her skin and tried to calm her active child. She winced from the pain in her ribs.

"He is active tonight." Her face was twisted with discomfort. She pulled the blanket closer around her.

"Has the evening's chill settled around you?"

"Let's sleep close to its warmth tonight. The heat may help to relax our child."

George moved the day bed close to the hearth and fitted it with several blankets and pillows. He filled the porch with wood and carried several armloads inside. When the iron ring was full, he placed a yule log to the side of the hearth to dry. He helped Mim settle into the night's bed and returned to the rocking chair. He was startled by a knock on his back door.

Mim threw the covers from her body and raced up the back staircase. George helped her enter the hidden room through the small raised panel. He heard the lock close as he exited the passageway. The pounding grew louder.

George opened the back door. Two men burst through its opening. Their eyes were wild. They chattered nervously.

"Are you George?"

"Who is asking?"

One man stepped forward. The brim of his worn leather hat shaded his face. George squinted in the dim light.

"We have traveled far. We have a message for a man named George."

"He is to live in this house."

George swallowed hard. Although he had proven his freedom several times, it was difficult to know how many bounty hunters and slave catchers had not received word that he was a free man; and then there was Mim.

"Follow me."

George led them into the sitting room. He opened the plantation desk drawer, slid his hand along the side, and opened a hidden hinge. A decorative medallion on the left side popped ajar. He gathered the string from around his neck and placed the gold key in his thick fingers. The lock obeyed, and George slid a small drawer from its concealed hiding spot. The men watched in awe. He unfolded a small stack of papers and handed them to the man closest to him. He read the pages in silence.

When the man finished reading the documents proving his freedom, George said, "I am he. I am George."

His smile was the only thing not shadowed by his brim. In one motion he removed his hat and held out his hand. "Pleased to make your acquaintance, George."

The second man stepped forward. He extended his hand and held a wax-sealed letter in the other. "We were asked to hand deliver this to George, although I must say I was startled. I was not expecting to be face to face with a freed slave."

George took the envelope from him. His face echoed his questions. He opened the wax seal without removing his eyes from his company. His heart raced as he read the contents:

George,

It is with mixed emotions I write this letter to you. In my hand I hold fifty dollars accompanying the request of freedom for one of my prized possessions. It is a difficult and curious time in which we live. The issue of slavery has escalated to an insurmountable height and I can no longer fight its wave. It has become impossible to continue our business without their aid. Our property lies in ruins. Our trusted men and women have fled or joined in the war effort with promise of freedom at its end. I see the smoke rising in the distance as well as within my own borders from a heinous march on Confederate soil.

This is not my war. It is not my fight. I am a simple businessman who spends his days toiling the unforgiving earth to yield a crop worth harvesting. I have spent my hard earned money to ensure the success of my land. I have sacrificed to give my group a safe place to live, work, and sleep. Even my heart was stolen by one of their own. To this I say I accept the money as payment for the freedom of my born property, Myra. May this find her in fine health and lifted spirit.

Master Barrisden
Springtide Cape

George suppressed a smile as he finished the letter before him. This was the first he had ever heard her master's name. He wondered if it was her first or second owner. He shook his head at the thought. The result is the issue.

The men eyed George as he lifted his head. They misinterpreted his head shaking.

"Do you know not of the named?"

"Sir?" Confused by their question, he narrowed his eyes.

"The one mentioned," the man tapped the letter, "have we delivered it to the wrong man? Are you not familiar with the name written within?" His voice was strained.

"Yes, I know the woman in which is mentioned."

"Woman?" he jumped. "Do you know where to find her?"

A hot flash moved through George's body. Suddenly uncertain if these men were friend or foe he became defensive. His staccato response took them by surprise.

"I...know...of a woman...so named. It will...take some...doing...to...locate her."

The men burst into laughter. George was not convinced. One of the men approached George and placed his hand on his shoulder.

"We come in peace, with news of freedom," he continued to laugh, "and you show fear? Rest easy, my friend, we are your brethren."

George relaxed his shoulders. His heart raced. His fist closed tightly around the news he had long desired. He offered the men a drink. They refused and slipped through the back door. He watched them ride away with their hands lifted in the moonlight in celebration. His relief came in tears.

He waited at the back door until the men and their horses had long disappeared. He read the letter once again. His thoughts were interrupted by the sound of a baby's cry. He ran up the back staircase taking three steps at a time. When he tapped on the raised panel, Mim did not reply. Panicked, he rattled the hidden door yet there was no reply.

"Mim!" his breaths were short and his words came in snorts. "Mim! Are you…?" The lock sprung open.

Mim sat on the floor in a puddle of blood. George rushed to her and the baby. He took the baby from her arms and wrapped it in his shirt. He gathered Mim from the floor. She moaned. He stared at the narrow opening of the raised panel and wondered how he would manage to move her through it. He whispered reassurances to her.

The opening was chest high. George struggled to move Mim's feet through the gap. He lifted her body and began to inch her through. With the narrowness of the passageway and the unforgiving space he had to maneuver, his body dripped with perspiration. All the while his thoughts were drowned by the baby's wails.

He envisioned Mim's slender legs crumpled against the wall of the duct, with her feet working as a wedge against forward progress. Her limp body made it difficult to guide. Her clothes were wet with water and blood. He struggled to hold her in the air. Exasperated he began to pull her back into the room. Her body was stuck.

In desperation, George screamed. The baby stopped crying, but Mim was unconscious. He positioned his body as close to the wall as possible and began to wiggle Mim's body until it started to move. He pushed her through the end of the passageway with ease as if someone carried her feet. Finally George was able to slide past her and pull her the rest of the way. He carried her to their bedroom and placed her on the bed.

He ran back to the panel, slid through the passageway, and entered the tiny room again. The baby was quiet. He lifted her in the air and carried the child to her mother's side.

Cool clean water filled the water basin. He dipped a towel until it was soaked, twisted it dry, and placed it on Mim's forehead. He gently patted his wife's cheek until she opened her eyes. He lifted her hips and placed several cloths beneath her. They were quickly soaked with her blood.

George's mind was wild with questions. He needed a doctor, but how could he leave Mim and the baby? With so much blood and a premature baby, George felt helpless. He knew they needed medical assistance. He whispered his intentions to Mim and rushed out of the house.

The frigid air rushed past his body leaving him unaffected by the cold. The sound of his horse pounding the frozen ground accentuated his frenzy. His bare hands were frozen to the reins, yet he did not notice the sting. His thoughts were on Mim and their baby. He could not shake the vision of her bloody dress, and his ears held the desperate cries from his child.

Lantern lights lit the doctor's house though the sight of its warmth did little to comfort him. He slid from his horse and pounded on the front door. When the doctor opened it, George blurted out his plea. The doctor grabbed his black bag and coat and jumped on the back of his unsaddled horse.

The bitter temperature made the layers of snow glisten like diamonds. A few stray flakes fell from the sky though no clouds were visible. Nerves gathered in George's chest making it difficult to breathe. He forced his mare to a faster gait.

George had long disappeared from the doctor's sight. He was forced to follow the tracks in the snow. His aging stallion struggled in the cold temperature making the doctor concerned he would reach his patients in time.

George jumped from his horse, neglecting to tie her, and called to Mim as he ran up the stairs. No reply came. Apprehensive to what may greet him he held his breath until he entered the room.

Mim's still body was positioned in a state of peaceful rest. The baby lay quietly against her rib. George whispered Mim's name. Only the baby stirred. He gathered the child in his arms and held Mim's hand.

"The doctor is on his way," he patted his wife's face. "Mim? Can you hear me?"

Tears moistened his face, "Mim?"

The doctor placed his bag on the floor, opened it, and pulled out a few instruments. He pointed to the basin. "You will need to bring fresh water, George." With his hands covered in blood he added, "A lot of water." George hesitated for a moment. "Go!" Distress punctuated his tone.

George carried the baby to the kitchen, wrapped her in a fresh cloth, and placed her in a crib. She began to cry. He rushed two pails of water to the doctor while the third began to heat on the wood stove. He added a few extra logs to speed up the process. After two more trips and four pails he brought the warm water to the doctor and was ushered from the room.

"Her bleeding has stopped. She is very weak though she holds out her arms for her child."

"She will...?" George could not force the balance of the question.

The doctor nodded in agreement. "She will be fine. Her recovery will be long and complicated with nursing."

"What can be done?" His question sounded alarms of exhaustion.

"I will send for a wet nurse. But for tonight, bring me Rebecca."

George was stunned at the name. "Rebecca?"

Slightly annoyed, the doctor questioned, "Did you not discuss the child's name?"

"Yes but...."

"Then bring me the child. Mim holds out her arms and whispers for her."

A shot of hot needles pricked George's body. He was unsure the doctor was correct. He picked up his daughter and carried her to Mim.

The doctor held out his arms. The baby wailed from the drop in temperature. He listened to her heartbeat, and checked her reflexes, eyes, mouth, and ears. He gathered and bound the bit of remaining umbilical cord.

"Her lungs are strong." He smiled for the first time.

George helped the doctor position Mim to nurse. The baby settled immediately. Mim's mumbled words could not be discerned.

After another hour the doctor was satisfied with her response. He gave George a specific list of care instructions for Mim and the baby and repeated them twice.

"I owe you my life. Thank you."

The doctor smiled, "It is what I do, George. Remember, she will be very weak. Her feet are not to touch the floor. I will send some help for the child. Prepare a room for your guest; she will be here for several days until Mim feels strong enough to try."

"Thank you, doctor," George hung his head. "I thought I might lose her."

"She is resilient. They both will be fine." He put on his hat and buttoned his cloak. "I will return tomorrow and perhaps the following day."

George nodded his head and thanked the doctor one last time. "Until tomorrow."

It was a long night. Sleep was not a thought for George. He held his child unless she was nursing and watched Mim as she slept. Her thoughts were restless and her words jumbled. The only one that was clear was the name *Rebecca*.

Mim opened her eyes for the first time as the noon hour approached the following day. As ordered, George prepared a cup of vegetable broth and offered it to his wife.

"The baby?"

"She is fine," he smiled. "She is with a nursemaid. Her appetite is great."

"Should she not be with me?"

"The doctor said you would insist. You need your rest and your strength. We will try in a few days." He held up the cup to her lips. "Drink this all. It will help you feel stronger."

Mim slept most of that day and the next. She woke the third day and insisted she try to nurse. George conceded but only once. By the fourth day the couple was alone. Mim joined them in the sitting room. The warmth of the fire was welcome.

It was nearly a week since the birth of their daughter. Mim gained strength each day and nursed with ease. George kept the fire burning and the kettle filled with stew. They sat together in silence and watched the flames lick the logs with color.

"What are your thoughts for her name?"

George looked at her puzzled. "You chose *Rebecca*."

Mim smiled at her husband. "I have chosen nothing."

"The doctor said you asked for her by name."

"By *Rebecca*?" She wrinkled her face.

"He said you held out your arms and called for Rebecca."

Mim gasped at his words. It was then she remembered her dream. "I dreamed of a young girl. Her hair was long and blonde. Her pink dress was adorned with lace and beads." Mim closed her eyes and rested her head on the back of the chair and continued. "She stood on a ridge. Autumn's splendor lit the background. She called for me, yet I could not reach her. Each step I walked pushed us farther apart. Her continuous motion coaxed me forward. A field of white lilies stood between us." Mim drew in a deep breath. "I can still smell their sweetness and feel their soft petals." She wiggled her fingers. "Finally, my body was able to move, and I walked to her side. We stood on a hill overlooking our home. '*They await your return,*' she spoke and pointed to our house." Mim held George's hand, "And when I opened my eyes I saw you."

His eyes were wide as she told her story. He had many questions, but uttered not one.

Mim asked quietly, "Was she *your Rebecca*?"

George felt a lump grow in his throat. He coughed to clear his voice.

"That was she." He took Mim's hand in both of his. "And what of a name?"

Mim picked up her sleeping daughter and kissed her face. She placed the bundle in George's arms. Her smile was wide.

"There can be only one name — *Rebecca*."

The toll of nearly losing Mim had settled deep inside him. That night George slept soundly for the first time in a week and dreamed.

At first George did not recognize the place in which he stood. He was surrounded by handmade gravestones, many fashioned with names, yet some bore only a modest cross. He swallowed hard when he realized he stood in the slaves' cemetery at Oak Bend. His eyes moved over the names written by his own hand. His vision was clouded with tears.

When he wiped his eyes George stood in Hope Cemetery. He found Rebecca crying at her parents' graves. An oak tree covered by a pink climbing rose stood as a sentry. Between their headstones was a barren patch of ground. Not a whisper of green could be found. It seemed Rebecca's tears salted the earth forbidding growth.

In the distance a young man wrapped in black sat still in a saddle. The wind tossed his cloak as his horse pawed at the ground. The air seemed anxious.

241

Rebecca ran to him. He reached for her and pulled her onto his saddle. Their bodies disappeared into a thick mist. George's feet were held fast to the ground. His hands held a heavy weight, but his eyes were darkened to its inscription. He forced his fingers to move over the marker's letters. He traced each one until he felt no more. Knowing the name, he hung his head and cried.

He woke in a cold sweat. Tears soaked his face. The evening's blazing fire was reduced to embers. No longer tired, he tossed another log onto the coals. He counted the chimes on each hour until light began to creep through the windowpanes.

George crossed his hands beneath his head. He watched the objects in the room slowly come into view. Mim and his daughter lay still in peaceful sleep. His thoughts calmed with the rise and fall of each breath.

Again, he thought of his dream. He thought of the barren ground, of Rebecca's tears, and her inability to find rest. He tried to focus on a solution, and then he remembered the weight of the marker in his hands. Peace filled him. Even with the absence of the boulder and the red Georgia soil, George knew what he must do next. It would be his last gift to her, the one that would be difficult, yet he would begin on this day.

believe...where Chattels continues.